"Can you still hike that kind of terrain? And when was the last time you rode a horse?"

"Nate McMann, I could outhike you any day of the week when we were in high school and you know it." The gall of the man! "And though I might not be able to break wild horses like you I can still ride with the best of them." She had no intention of telling him that she hadn't ridden a horse in nine years!

"I never said you couldn't ride or hike," he said. His tone sent shivers through her. Confused her.

The man still got to her. There was absolutely no denying that. It was maddening and crazy. But, maybe this was what she needed. Maybe this was the thing that would clear the air once and for all.

Alaskan Bride Rush:
Women are flocking to the Land of the
Midnight Sun with marriage on their minds

Books by Debra Clopton

Love Inspired

*The Trouble with
  Lacy Brown
*And Baby Makes Five
*No Place Like Home
*Dream a Little Dream
*Meeting Her Match
*Operation:
  Married by Christmas
*Next Door Daddy
*Her Baby Dreams

*The Cowboy Takes a Bride
*Texas Ranger Dad
*Small-Town Brides
  "A Mule Hollow Match"
*His Cowgirl Bride
**Her Forever Cowboy
**Cowboy For Keeps
Yukon Cowboy

*Mule Hollow
**Men of Mule Hollow

DEBRA CLOPTON

was a 2004 Golden Heart finalist in the inspirational category, a 2006 Inspirational Readers' Choice Award winner, a 2007 Golden Quill award winner and a finalist for the 2007 American Christian Fiction Writers Book of the Year Award. She praises the Lord each time someone votes for one of her books, and takes it as an affirmation that she is exactly where God wants her to be.

Debra is a hopeless romantic and loves to create stories with lively heroines and the strong heroes who fall in love with them. But most important, she loves showing her characters living their faith, seeking God's will in their lives one day at a time. Her goal is to give her readers an entertaining story that will make them smile, hopefully laugh and always feel God's goodness as they read her books. She has found the perfect home for her stories, writing for the Love Inspired line, and still has to pinch herself just to see if she really is awake and living her dream.

When she isn't writing, she enjoys taking road trips, reading and spending time with her two sons, Chase and Kris. She loves hearing from readers and can be reached through her Web site, www.debraclopton.com, or by mail at P.O. Box 1125, Madisonville, Texas 77864.

Yukon Cowboy
Debra Clopton

Steeple
Hill®

Published by Steeple Hill Books™

Special thanks and consideration to Debra Clopton for her participation in the Alaskan Bride Rush series.

STEEPLE HILL BOOKS

Steeple
Hill®

Recycling programs
for this product may
not exist in your area.

ISBN-13: 978-0-373-81504-3

YUKON COWBOY

Copyright © 2010 by Harlequin Books S.A.

Printed in U.S.A.

The Lord is good, a refuge in times of trouble.
He cares for those who trust in him.
—Nahum 1:7

This book is dedicated to Ms. Jo. You are truly an inspiration and a blessing to me and all those whose lives you touch.

Chapter One

"You want me to assist in a *tour?*" Bethany Marlow asked, in disbelief. Surely her friend and ex-boss was joking. "You're kidding, right?"

"No kidding involved," Amy James said, and though she was smiling, the petite, blonde owner of Alaska's Treasures tour company looked like she wasn't taking no for an answer. "I'm so glad you've chosen to move back to Treasure Creek and open a wedding-planning business. It is going to be a wonderful addition to the town. I know I'm springing this on you, and probably before you've even unpacked your suitcase. I'm desperate, though. This is a family tour that I feel needs a woman guide assisting the lead guide."

Bethany couldn't believe her ears. Her plane had landed barely an hour ago—and yes, her bags were still packed. She'd been in such a hurry to get outside and not waste any of the precious Alaskan daylight that she'd simply slid them inside her hotel room and hurried outside. She'd been stopped several times by acquaintances who were as excited to see her as she was them. Seeing her old friend Amy coming toward her lifted her spirits even higher. But help lead a tour? This was the last thing she had expected to hear from Amy. She hadn't led a tour in years. The idea was kind of tempting, however, opening her wedding-planning business had to come first.

"Amy," she said, feeling bad, "I'd like to help, but I have to put finding a spot to open my store first."

Amy smiled, her eyes twinkling. "Got that covered already. There's a space that opened up around the corner from The General Store just off of Main Street. It's just the cutest, quaintest storefront, with personality plus. I can see your name on the window right now. The location is great. Not that it will matter—as soon as these women hear you're in town, I have a feeling you'll be overrun with clients."

"My word, Amy, you're like a steam-roller!" Bethany laughed—more from surprise than anything. "You've been thinking ahead on this curveball you've thrown me." She sobered. "And all before I've even had time to tell you how sorry I was to hear about Ben. I am really so sorry." Amy's husband, Ben had died in a tragic accident just a few short months ago. His death left Amy to raise their two young sons on her own, plus running the tour company business, Alaska's Treasures, by herself. "You have a lot sitting on your shoulders. How are you holding up?"

The entire town was reliant on the tour company to bring in the visitors that kept the town going. Tourist trade was the primary support for all the businesses in town.

"It has to have been so hard on you. I can't imagine."

Amy pushed her red curls from her face with one hand, a softness coming to her eyes. "It has been hard, but God's been right there beside me. And the people of Treasure Creek—oh, Bethany—they have just been wonderful. There isn't a better bunch of people in all of the world."

"I agree," Bethany said, and meant it. She'd met some nice people in San Francisco and on her trips around the country, but her heart had a special fondness toward the people of her hometown. She'd missed them. Not that it really was her hometown. Her dad's job in the oil industry had transplanted them into the community when she was in elementary school, but she claimed it as her own. Sadly, she hadn't really appreciated it until she'd moved away and been gone for a while.

"So, will you help out and take the tour? It will be good for you. Like getting your feet wet again with the way of life here in town. You'll be getting in touch with your roots."

"You make it hard to say no."

"I try. Ever since that *Now Woman* magazine article came out about all the hunky tour guides working for me, the tour business has really picked up. It's just been a blessing to everyone. And not just single women are coming to town looking for love, but also the family tours are picking up, too. Why don't you do this? The reason I need you so much is that the family on the tour has just adopted the little boy they've been foster parents to. They really could use your help. The mom is nervous about the trip and feels like a woman guide will help her feel more at ease."

Amy was watching her intently. She was the type of person who'd always tried to take care of everyone around her. She was still doing it. Bethany knew there was no way she could refuse to help her friend. She'd worked as an assistant guide all through high school. It had been a while, but she was pretty sure she still had what it took to get the job done. At least she liked to think that she still had it. She might have moved to the big city, but she hadn't gone soft.

Plus, Amy was right. The article had been a blessing to everyone, even her. If it hadn't been for Amy's interview with the *Now Woman* writer, Bethany would still be back in San Francisco, growing more dissatisfied by the minute with the way her life was going. The article had been about how gorgeous and wonderful all the eligible bachelors were who worked for Alaska's Treasures tour company. It had shocked Bethany at first—not the hunky bachelor part, since she knew all too well how true that part was—but it had shocked her that Amy had given an interview about them like that. It hadn't seemed like Amy. Talking about her love for her town and her tour company, now that was Amy. Bethany had learned later from her mom who'd heard it through the grapevine that the reporter had given the article "the bachelor twist" all on her own. Romance sold articles, and it had also sold the town. Interest picked up;

women were everywhere, coming to town in the hope of falling in love and getting married ever since. Reading it herself had brought tears to Bethany's eyes, and she had to come. It was the answer to her prayers.

After all, where there were weddings there needed to be a wedding planner, and she just happened to be a very good one.

Being home did have its problems though—namely, Nate McMann.

Her heart skipped a couple of beats at the thought of him. After all these years and all that had happened, how was that? Unfortunately, it was inevitable that she'd run into him. Treasure Creek was small. She wondered what it would be like to see him again. She'd heard that he had never married—but she wasn't going to think about that. Instead she focused on Amy. "Maybe you're right. Maybe I do need to get in touch with my roots. I have missed the wilderness. There is nothing to compare to the beauty of Alaska in the raw."

Amy looked pleased. "So you'll do it?"

Excitement hit her. "Sure, why not," she

said, with gusto. "If the guys are still as rough as they used to be, then I'd feel guilty if I leave that poor mother to make it on her own," she said, laughing.

"Oh, they are that. Although you know as well as I do that there is more marshmallow beneath most of their thick skin."

Bethany had learned that with many of the older guides she'd helped out during high school. But she wondered about the guys who'd been her age. Specifically, she wondered about Nate—it was something she was going to have to stop doing. She'd heard that he'd taken over running the family ranch when his father retired. She knew from the hours his dad had worked that it was a full-time job. That meant she could relax. It was highly improbable that Nate was a guide any longer. Even in high school, he'd been part-time because of the demands of the ranch.

"Count me in," she said. "Will I have time to get the space leased and then get my gear together before this tour leaves?"

"This is wonderful!" Amy exclaimed.

"You have two days before the tour heads out, and everything except clothes will be packed and ready for you. Can you come by the office tomorrow for a briefing?"

"Sure."

What was she doing?

"And no worries about the shop. I'm sure before the sun goes down you'll have a lease on that space. I'm telling you, it is perfect. You run on over there now and look. I'll give Maxine at the real estate office a call, so she can head in that direction and meet you there."

"Hold on," Bethany laughed. "You never told me who was leading the tour or where it's going."

Amy already had her cell phone out and pressed to her ear—"I'm still juggling the guys around because of all the honeymoons we've been working into the schedules. Oh, hi, Maxine, this is Amy James, how are you today?" Nodding at something Maxine was saying, Amy cupped her hand over the phone and whispered, "Go on now. Maxine will be there in a few. Come see me tomorrow for a briefing at ten, and I'll get you filled in on everything— Yes, Maxine, I'm still here." She waved toward the direction of the office and mouthed the word *go.*

Bethany did as she was told.

How had this happened? She was home, she was on the scent of the perfect office space and she was booked on an Alaskan wilderness tour—all thanks to Amy. And she hadn't even been back in Treasure Creek for an hour. Her head was spinning. People thought life in a small town moved slowly—obviously they hadn't been in Treasure Creek lately.

She hadn't gone but a few steps around the corner when she saw him. Tall, broad-shouldered and as strikingly handsome as he'd always been, Nate McMann was coming out of The General Store with a box of candy in his hand. He wore a rugged sheepskin jacket, his thick blond hair showing beneath his tan Stetson. She'd always loved his hair.

Her footsteps faltered and her heart began

pounding, banging against her chest double-time at the sight of him.

He was the most handsome man she'd ever seen—nothing about him had changed. From the shadow of his Stetson, his blue, blue eyes locked onto hers.

She couldn't breathe.

How was it that the man who'd broken her heart into a thousand pieces could still cause her to go weak in the knees?

It was pathetic…then again, she guessed weak in the knees was okay as long as she didn't go weak in the brain.

She had no intention of doing that. She'd become strong and independent in the last few years. It hadn't been easy, though. After he'd sent her away, she'd had to strong-arm herself out of the fog of longing and hurt before it got the better of her.

And now, here she was standing in the middle of town gawking at him and feeling as vulnerable as a kitten.

She needed to act.

To *do* something.

Say something. But what?

She focused on the positives. Thanks to Nate, she hadn't just talked about her dreams, she'd gone for them and achieved everything she set out to do—funny how things had worked out.

"Hello, Nate," she said, just as casually as she greeted every other old friend she met strolling down the street. It sounded good. Strong. Self-confident. Unhurt. In control.

He shifted from one boot to the other.

His eyes, the color of the Pacific Ocean washed over her. Was it her imagination that, for an instant, she thought he'd been drinking in the sight of her as she'd done with him? Foolish was what that was. She wouldn't let *that* thought cross her mind again. "Bethany," he said quietly. "Hi."

She always loved the way he said her name. There was something so gentle in the sound, coming from such a rugged man. It had always made her feel protected and... *special* to him. *What a lie that had been,* she thought, with a jolt of reality. "You look *great*." She wanted to kick herself for blurting out the first thing that came to mind. But she felt like a schoolgirl again, all uncertain and nervous. It was horrible.

"So do you," he said, dropping the ribbon-tied box of chocolates to his side. Her gaze followed it.

He had a woman in his life, it seemed.

"Why are you back in Treasure Creek?"

Bethany almost laughed. Everyone in town more than likely knew why she was back by the time her flight landed. They probably even knew that she was walking down the street at this very minute and was now stopped, talking to her old boyfriend.

"You haven't heard?" she asked, dismayed, feeling like every moment standing there with him was endless.

"I heard that you're opening a wedding-planning service." His gaze sharpened, pinned her like blue darts. "*Why* is what I'm asking. You don't belong here."

His harsh statement cut like a sharp wind, sending a chill up her spine. What was his problem? This was the man who'd told her in one breath he loved her, wanted to spend his life with her, and then the next breath took it back. All these years, what had happened between them still made no sense to her, and he had the *gall* to tell her she didn't belong here. Fine, maybe she didn't, but she was here.

And this time, if she left it would be because she truly wanted to. And if she left, it would be with her chin held high…and her heart intact.

She sucked in a steadying breath. "I'm not sure why you think that." She managed to sound unaffected. "But I can tell you that it's not something you need to spend any time concerning yourself over. My being here won't affect your life in the least. Nice seeing you, Nate," she offered the last as she sidestepped him. A lady she didn't know was coming out of the store and Bethany slipped through the open door. Her knees were rattling against each other as the door closed behind her. It was all she could do not to turn and see if he was watching her. The tingle at the back of her neck told her he was.

Of all the scenarios that had gone through her mind about what their first meeting would be like, this wasn't one of them. Awkward and tough was what that had been—but then, she'd been kidding herself, if she expected anything else.

Nate hadn't had a good night as he pulled his truck to a stop in front of Alaska's Treasures, the tour company where he led a few tours a month. Normally, on a day like today, when he was heading in for a briefing before his tour, he was in a great mood, looking forward to the trek out into wilderness he loved.

Not today.

Today he was too preoccupied with other things.

He slammed his truck door just as a gust of October wind bit at him. Jerking the brim of his Stetson low against his forehead, he was unable to stop himself from glancing down the street. Where *was* she?

He'd heard yesterday that she was arriving, and he should have stayed out of town.

But he'd had to get birthday candy for Sue, his housekeeper. In and out had been the plan, with no expectation of running into Bethany. His legs went weak at the thought of seeing her.

When he'd looked up and locked gazes with her it was like seeing a mirage. Like she'd always done, she took his breath away. She'd had the greenest eyes—like translucent green glass, they sparkled and captured the light and held it. He'd always gotten lost peering into their depths. And her dark hair, straight and shiny—just like he'd remembered—framed her heart-shaped face…the same sweet face that had haunted his dreams for nearly a decade.

He closed his eyes and tried to ease the turmoil that rumbled inside of him.

Why did she come home to Treasure Creek?

The question had been eating at him ever since word had gotten out that she was returning. He didn't understand it and hadn't believed it at first. She'd had big dreams and wanted to leave Treasure Creek and pursue them more than anything when they were in high school. She'd had the grit to make those dreams reality, too…so why was she here now?

He knew all about the wedding-planning business she was supposed to be opening, but like he'd told her, that didn't explain *why*. Why had she given up her dream job in San Francisco to open up a shop here in Treasure Creek? It didn't make sense. That was for certain.

He hadn't handled seeing her very well. Ever since their encounter, he felt like he'd been trampled beneath the hooves of a herd of stampeding cattle.

He needed this tour. He'd been too busy at the ranch over the last couple of months to take one out, and he was chomping at the bit to get out there on the trails. For more reasons than to get away from Bethany. He needed to do his part in helping find the treasure that the town was searching for.

Ever since Ben James, owner of the tour company, had died, the town had struggled economically. The tour company brought in most of the revenue for the town, and things had not been the same since Ben had passed.

Amazingly, an old treasure map that belonged to Amy's great, great grandfather, Mack Tanner, had been discovered after years of merely being a rumor. The discovery had thrown Nate for a loop, because his grandfather had died almost fifteen years ago searching for the stupid treasure—a fact that had torn Nate up all these years. Realizing that his grandfather actually might have died for more than just a rumor didn't make him any less fond of the idea of a real treasure, but if there actually was one, and it could help the town, then it was worth something. The town had high hopes of finding it.

Nate still had his doubts that the treasure existed; however, if it did, he wanted a crack at finding it. And he wanted this tour because of its location.

Amy was sending the treasure map out with the guides so that they could check different locations, in the hope of finding the right one. He was leading this family tour on a five-day excursion that would go past the place where his grandfather had died. It wasn't a place he was fond of…Nate had almost died there himself. He'd been on a mission to figure out what his grandfather had seen before he'd fallen from the mountain.

After his near-fatal slip, and almost following in his grandfather's footsteps, he'd never gone back…until now. This time things would go better. He was determined to find out what his grandfather had found inside the crevice two hundred feet up the face of that cold, ragged rock.

He welcomed the trip more today than yesterday. Today he needed something to focus his anger and disillusionment on.

Glowering, ready for distraction right at that very instant, he stalked up the sidewalk toward the "log cabin" office that housed the tour company. It was nice to see a buzz of activity humming about it, as people came and went out the door. He tipped his hat when a gaggle of women walked past, ogling him like a slab of bacon. He preferred to ignore them, but for the sake of the town he'd play the friendly cowboy role and tip the Stetson and show hospitality. As long as everyone in town understood that tipping his hat was as far as it went with him in letting these bride wannabes try to hook him as a husband. He'd already had a dolled-up redhead named Delilah pull two crazy cons on him. The woman had cornered him in Lizbet's Diner and asked him if he was alone. Of course he'd said yes, because he was. If he'd known she was going to plunk herself into the booth with him and invite herself to lunch, he'd have said he was leaving.

He didn't even want to *think* about the second time she'd cornered him. It was enough to make a man walk off into the wilderness and never come back.

"Hey, Nate," Gage Parker called, falling into step beside him. Gage was a tour guide and also a member of the search and rescue team.

"Any luck finding Tucker Lawson?"

Nate asked, not breaking step. Tucker was a former local. He'd moved away after a rift with his dad but recently his dad had passed away. Tucker had come in for the funeral then disappeared. His best friend Jake Rodgers was funding an ongoing search for him that Gage and police chief Truscott were heading up.

"Nothing new since I saw you last week. We've been out a few more times but we can only hope he's found refuge somewhere…if he's alive."

"There's always a chance." Nate knew as well as Gage that every day that passed was a bad sign. There was no need to state that. "Everyone is still praying for him."

"Tucker needs every one of them," Gage said, studying him. "I'll be driving your group to the drop point out at Chilkoot Trail day after tomorrow."

"That'll be good," Nate grunted, sliding him a glance. Gage looked happy. He was glad someone was. Gage had recently fallen in love with Karenna, a nice girl who'd fallen for all this craziness about finding a husband in this town. Crazy as it was, something good had come out of all of this.

"You look about as happy as that cougar you had to rescue out of that tank last week," Gage said, matching him step for step. "You've seen her, haven't you?"

There was no use pretending he didn't know who "her" was. Everyone would be speculating on the same question, and he had no doubt he'd be asked it by every person he met—especially his fellow tour guides. He figured, since he'd run into Bethany on the street in front of The General Store, that someone would have seen them and that the grapevine would be alive by now.

"Yes, I've seen her," he said, sliding Gage a look that hopefully told him to back off. Yeah, right.

Gage grinned. "Mom was shopping in town and saw you run into each other in front of The General Store. She said it was about as awkward as two porcupines in a box together. She also said Nadine rented

Bethany that vacant building around the corner from the store." Gage turned toward town and pointed. "That one. The one you can just see the front of from here. You know, where Frank Drew had that lousy bakery."

Nate spun and stared toward the shop. The front door was visible from this angle, though the rest of the stores on the side street were blocked from view. As he stared, she actually came outside. Even from this distance she could push his buttons. He swallowed hard and told his feet to march straight inside and not to look back.

"She's still as pretty as ever," Gage said.

Despite not wanting to have this conversation, Nate's feet wouldn't move. "Yeah, she is," he admitted. "She really rented the space?" It was a stupid question, since Gage had just said the words.

"Looks like she's staying."

It did. She *really* was staying. Nate reached for the door when he preferred to head for his truck. Instead of pulling it open he let go, snatched his hat from his head and rammed his hand through his hair. *Bethany always liked his hair.*

The thought came out of nowhere, like so many others had the night before. He'd ridden a horse for hours after he'd gotten home to the ranch yesterday. But nothing had stopped the memories from tearing him apart.

"Are you all right?" Gage asked.

"Yeah, I'm fine." It was a flat-out lie. He knew it and so did Gage.

"You know I've never been one to pry, but this could turn out to be a good thing, Nate."

Nate shot him a scowl. "I'm not going to worry about it. She'll do her thing and I'll do mine."

"Good luck with that." Gage grinned and headed down the sidewalk. Nate watched him go, trying to get his thoughts together. She wouldn't stay. She had wanted to leave too much when they were in high school. She was here for a reason he didn't understand. But one thing was certain…he wasn't all right, and he wouldn't be until she hopped back on a plane and headed back to her life and her dreams. The ones he'd wanted her to have more than anything.

Even more than his own dreams.

Chapter Two

Feeling almost giddy with expectations, Bethany stood out in front of her new space and studied the whitewashed, planked siding. She loved it. Amy had been so completely right. The space was perfect, and Bethany had rented it on the spot.

There was an office area and plenty of room for her to display the various props and wares she offered when planning and staging a wedding. It was just around the corner from Main Street, and there was an apartment above it for rent, too. She wasn't sure how long she'd stay in Treasure Creek, only time would tell; but right now she had a great feeling about it—despite her less than promising meeting with Nate the day before.

Hopefully, time would fix the strain their past cast on them, but for now she wasn't going to dwell on it. She'd awakened feeling refreshed and excited about being in Treasure Creek. She was even thrilled about helping lead the family tour.

But getting her shop up and running was her first priority. She'd called the electric and phone service and those utilities would be on by the time she returned from the tour. Her things should have arrived by then, too. It wouldn't take long to set up after that, once she knew how she wanted things placed. Walking back inside, she placed her hands on her hips and surveyed the long, narrow space. It had promise. The tour would keep her from getting impatient. She hated waiting.

From the look of things, she wasn't going to be able to get unpacked quickly enough. There had already been five women who'd come by and made appointments for consultations. She was flying by the seat of her pants, using a wooden crate as a reception desk and a piece of notebook paper as an appointment book. These women were ready to get married.

She checked her watch. She needed to be at the tour company in less than fifteen minutes for her briefing. Amy had assured her that everything she needed would be packed and ready for her when they left, and all she needed to worry about were her jeans and tops. Boots, jackets, food and sleeping bags would all be ready. She smiled at that. After packing to come home to Treasure Creek, the last thing she wanted to do was pack some more. It was an easy plan, and she was really glad she'd agreed to go.

Yes, opening the shop was a priority, but there was just something about being back in Alaska that called her to the wilds of the breathtaking frontier.

She folded the paper with appointments on it, and was about to stick it in her purse when the door opened.

"Knock, knock. Anybody in here?" a

sweet Southern voice with a raspy edge to it called.

Bethany turned to find a blonde of about forty peek her head through the cracked door.

"Well, hi-dee! There you are, standing in the dark!"

"Hi," Bethany said, moving forward. The woman was smiling wide and warm and was as pretty as Dolly Parton. She even reminded Bethany of the country singer, with the cute way she'd greeted her and the smile that took over her heart-shaped face. And her big, blond hair was poofed and sprayed as heavy as any of Dolly's styles. Bethany had worked with many, many wealthy mothers of the bride who'd looked just as overly coifed. Usually, she had the insane urge to sink her fingers into the stiff dos and shake hair loose from the lacquer holding it in place. Like all those other times though, she curbed the insane thought and held out her hand. "I'm Bethany. Can I help you?"

"Oh, honey, I hope so. Are you the

new wedding planner?" she drawled, flushing slightly, as if embarrassed about something.

"That's me," Bethany said brightly.

"That's just wonderful. I'm Joleen Jones," she gushed. Extending a perfectly manicured hand, she shook Bethany's hand gently. "I can't tell you how excited I was to find that you were coming to town. I'm here to talk about my wedding plans."

Bethany couldn't help smiling at the cute lilt to her voice. "That's great. I'm not officially opened and I have to be at the tour company in a few moments—"

"I understand. This won't take a minute. I was hoping to get an appointment on the books."

Bethany couldn't say no, so she set her purse down and opened the paper where she'd been writing the brides' and grooms' names down. It was exciting to see business going great guns, even before there was a stick of furniture in the place. "I'll set you up with an appointment for when I get back in town. I'm actually leaving on Wednesday to help out with a tour—I used to work for Amy James in high school, and I'm going to help out for a few days while I wait for my things to arrive." She wasn't sure why she was explaining so much, but the look in the woman's eyes had her wanting to put her at ease about as much as she could. "You said your name was Joleen Jones. And the groom?" She wrote her name on the page. When Joleen didn't say anything Bethany looked up and asked again, thinking she hadn't spoken loudly enough, "And the groom is…?"

Joleen looked sheepishly at her, with big, long-lashed, amber eyes. "Harry Peters."

The name was almost a whisper, but it had Bethany's ears perked up. *Harry Peters!* "From The General Store?" she clarified, thinking, surely Joleen had said something similar to Harry's name and she'd misunderstood. This woman and Harry were as far from what she would have ever matched up as any two people she'd ever worked with.

Joleen nodded. "Isn't he the cutest thing you ever saw?"

Well, there you go—love was the weirdest thing sometimes. Bethany grinned, feeling Joleen's delight roll over to her. "Congratulations. I think that is wonderful," she said, sincerely.

"I just came to town a few weeks ago and he has just been so helpful. He is really a dear. Don't you think so?"

"Always. When is the wedding date?" Pen poised to write she waited for the answer.

Joleen placed a long, red fingernail on her bottom lip and hesitated. "Um, there isn't a date set. Yet. He hasn't asked me out yet, you see. But I'm sure that he will." Her words had started out hesitantly, but she ended in a rush, as if she were trying to convince herself of the fact. This was odd... two-in-a-row odd. There had been a lady in earlier, asking about planning a wedding for Christmas. That fancily dressed lady, Delilah Carrington, also hadn't had a groom. But she was different than Joleen, she hadn't set her sights on anyone in particular yet. Oh no, Delilah was shopping the field and ready to pounce on whomever proposed first. She'd set a deadline for herself to be married by Christmas, and she'd come to Treasure Creek to fulfill that deadline. She struck Bethany as the type who would get what she wanted. It was crazy, but it might be fun watching her in action.

Bethany certainly wasn't here to judge anyone, her job was just to plan beautiful weddings and carry them off with grace and expertise.

"He hasn't asked you out?" she asked, because she couldn't come up with anything better to ask. And she was curious and hoping Joleen would explain.

Joleen bit her upper lip and blushed. "No. But it's because he's shy that way. I guess I'm jumping the gun here, trying to get an appointment. This probably sounds a little crazy, doesn't it? No, wait, don't answer that. I *know* it sounds crazy."

"No," Bethany began, then got honest,

"actually it does…a little, but I've seen stranger things."

Joleen smiled in relief and relaxed. "I guess I am ahead of myself. I…I do want you to know I will be using you sometime in the near future, though. Harry is sure to come around."

Bethany's heart tugged at the angst she could hear in Joleen's voice. She knew all too well how it felt to love a man and not be able to have the happy ending she want— *stop!* She snatched her purse and forced her smile wide. "Joleen, I'm here when you need me. And as soon as I get up and running, you come by anytime you want and we'll get details perfected, so when your special man does pop the question you'll be all set. It takes time to get all the details right, so nothing says you can't already be working on your special day."

Her positive words must have seemed like music as they hit Joleen's ears. She straightened, and a warm smile that was free of any hesitation blossomed across her pretty face. "You really wouldn't think me too crazy to do that? I mean Harry, the sweet man, is just a bit slow on the uptake—if you know what I mean. He does care for me. I've seen the way he looks at me when he thinks I'm not looking. He's the strong, silent type."

Bethany almost choked. "I don't think you're crazy at all. Hey, I'm a romantic through and through, and this is very romantic, if you ask me. Harry Peters is a lucky man to have you, and he'd be smart to open his eyes and ask you out." It was the truth. That dry piece of toast needed a gal like Joleen to top off his life like sweet jam.

Joleen startled her by embracing her in a big hug. "Thank you. You have absolutely made my day."

"You've made mine. It was really nice meeting you," she said, and meant it. As they parted and headed in opposite directions, Bethany hoped Joleen got her happy ending. Glancing over her shoulder, she watched Joleen round the corner and walk daintily toward The General Store. Bethany suddenly wished she were a fly on the wall so she could see the grumpy Harry Peters's face when Joleen was around.

Before she realized what she was doing, she said a prayer that Harry would be the hero in Joleen's life. It would be nice if the Lord chose to work that out for her.

She continued on toward the tour company, glancing across the street at the quaint church where children played in the playground. Bethany had spent many Sundays sitting beside Nate on the second-from-last pew of that church. Since moving from Treasure Creek, she'd not been in church on a regular basis. Her faith, like her heart, had taken a hit when Nate had told her he didn't love her, and that she shouldn't hang around town because of him.

Bethany's dreams back then had conflicted with one another. She'd wanted to be successful in her own right as a wedding planner, and she'd wanted Nate. And she'd wanted children with Nate. In her naivety, she'd thought she could have it all. But there weren't many weddings in Treasure Creek before the article.

Now she was just looking to have a lovely life. She wanted satisfaction and fulfillment. She wanted…something elusive that she hadn't found with her career in San Francisco. Sure, she'd flown to Italy and Australia and other places to carry off the weddings of wealthy clients for the firm she'd worked for, and loved every minute of it. But now, at twenty-nine, with no husband and no children, she knew she wanted more. And she hoped that more was here in Treasure Creek.

She wanted to know that God had a plan for her life—a plan that she would understand soon. Maybe, being back in Treasure Creek, she'd find the faith she once had. The faith to believe that God really did have her in the palm of His hand.

A prayer for Joleen was a start.

Out in the wilderness, she'd always felt closer to God. Who wouldn't? Maybe out there she'd feel the peace she'd missed.

"Nate, I want you to look around the cabin at point three on your tour, but I really don't want you going to Klink's Ridge," Amy said, from across the desk in her office. "We both know no good can come of that. And if by some stretch of the imagination the treasure is in there, then it will just have to stay there, unless you find another entrance. I can't imagine my great, great grandfather scaling the wall to hide something in such a dangerous place."

Nate ran a finger along the crease of his cowboy hat. He planned to scale that ridge and find the cave that his grandfather had believed held the treasure. He'd tried it once and almost fallen to his death, just like his grandfather had. But Nate had made a careless mistake. He wouldn't make that mistake again. He'd been thinking about it, and felt he owed it to his grandfather to figure out if he'd discovered anything before he plunged down the face of that cliff. Amy didn't need to worry herself about it, though, so he kept his plans to himself.

"I'll be checking around the cabin. When you showed me the map I realized—because the map leads me to believe the treasure is buried near a cabin—that maybe my grandfather thought the same thing. This opening on the face of Klink's Ridge may be a cave opening he thought linked to a cave. I'm not sure what my grandfather was thinking. I may never know. But I'm going with my gut here and checking all this out."

Amy nodded. "There are just some things in life only God knows the reasons for."

Nate's thoughts went instantly to the day he heard the doctor tell him he would never father children. After a mild case of the measles—despite his childhood vaccine—Nate had been shocked when his dad suggested the doctor test him during his checkup. He'd been nineteen, and when the test revealed that he was sterile his world had changed. He'd gone from being a man with everything to a man with nothing in an instant, knowing there was no way on earth he would be able to look Bethany in the eye and ask her to marry him. Why had this happened to him? He'd asked himself and God that question over and over again… with no answer.

God's reasoning wasn't something he thought about much anymore. He still went to church on occasion, just because in Treasure Creek it was expected. He'd be considered a heathen for certain if he never stepped foot in the church…and maybe yes, there was a possibility that he might hear something from the preacher that helped him process the reasoning behind his inability to give the woman he loved the children she wanted so badly. Even now the thought made him ache through and through.

"I've found the perfect guide to help you with this tour group."

Amy's soft voice broke into his deep thoughts and he pulled back from the mental road he'd been traveling on—it was a road that led him nowhere good. He was glad to have something else to think about. Before Bethany had come home, he'd pressed any longing for her he had deep into the most hidden recesses of his being so that he was able to cope. Coping. It was a double life he lived, but knowing she was living her dreams helped him. Now that she was here, coping was going to be a killer.

"Who's going with me?" he asked. He liked all the younger tour guides. Most were just out of high school, ready to learn as much as possible so they could begin leading their own tours. None of them had ever been as great to have along as Bethany had been…she'd always given the tours a good twist. Her insights into the country and the animal life always added a fun element.

"The Taylors have adopted this little boy, and he's pretty rambunctious and has a few attention problems. They requested a female guide to help lead the tour, because the mother felt she would be more comfortable, given the situation."

Nate wasn't surprised to have an extra guide on a family tour, especially since he was going to take a few private excursions in the hopes of finding the treasure. But a woman—who? The only woman guide they had at the moment was Casey Donner, and she was already out in the field. At least he thought so. "Who? Did Casey get back in early?"

"No. It's someone new." Amy tapped her pencil on the table, then let it drop as she pushed her chair back and got up.

She was acting differently. What was up, he wondered, as she crossed to the door, cracked it open and peeked out into the waiting area then closed the door. The last thing he wanted on this tour was to be breaking in a wet-behind-the-ears woman.

Turning, she settled serious eyes on him. "Okay, she's here now. This is going to be great, Nate. Remember, I'm doing what is best for this family, and I expect you to do the same. Here at Alaska's Treasures tour company we always think of the clients first."

Nate wasn't sure how to take Amy's tone or the look on her face. But her words had his stomach feeling suddenly like hot mush. "Amy, what have you done—" he started, but she opened the door and beckoned someone inside.

The last someone he'd ever expected to see walk through that door as a tour guide. Bethany.

Chapter Three

Bethany walked into Amy's office and stopped in her tracks. Nate jerked to his feet so fast, he sent his chair sliding into the bookcase behind it as he gasped in horror.

What had she done to make this man change toward her like he had?

"Amy," she snapped, her temper at his attitude spiking. "I'm not sure I understand—or like this one bit."

Nate positively glowered at Amy, looking like he could wring her neck. The man obviously had a problem, and it looked like Bethany was it.

Unaffected by either of them, Amy smiled breezily, as if Nate looked at her that way all the time. She drew Bethany into the room and closed the door. "Look, I didn't think either of you would understand this. That's why I chose not to tell you what I'd done until now. But, Bethany, the minute I heard you were coming to town I knew you both would be the perfect guides for this family tour. Remember, I've seen you work together before—you were the best team ever. And this family needs a compassionate woman like you along, Bethany. You are an answer to a prayer, coming back at the time that you did. I wasn't sure what I was going to do. And they also need you, Nate, because I believe you have something to offer the little boy. He is seven years old, his name is Cody, and he needs strong male role models in his life. You are that in every sense of the word—" she dropped her chin to her chest and lifted a brow "—when you aren't looking as if you just stepped barefoot into a pot of boiling water."

At that, his jaw jerked and he started to say something. Amy held up her hand. "You can help this little boy by being a positive role model to him. Believe me, I'm so thankful that Ben's and my sons have so many of you men around to show them how to be good, strong Christian men. That's what you can do on this trip."

Bethany glanced at Nate. Nate glanced at her.

How could either of them refuse that?

This was not good. Bethany wanted to leave. She wanted to stay. She *wanted* to know what Nate's problem was.

He thumped his hat against his thigh, looking like a trapped grizzly.

"I'll do it," she said. She wasn't so sure about being an answer to a prayer, but if there was a chance she could help this little boy by being a kind and compassionate guide, then she would. Nate would just have to deal with it. Especially since it looked like he wasn't going to be any of those things.

"I'm in, too," he grunted, making his way past her to the door. He stopped beside her. "Can you still hike that kind of terrain?

And when was the last time you rode a horse?"

"Nate McMann, I could outhike you any day of the week when we were in high school, and you know it." The gall of the man! "*And* though I might not be able to break wild horses like you can, I can still ride with the best of them." She had no intention of telling him that she hadn't ridden a horse in nine years. Oh, no, she'd sit in that saddle like she'd been riding every day, just so she'd have the satisfaction of wiping that condescension off his face.

"I never said you couldn't ride or hike," he said, his tone sent shivers through her. Confused her. "We have our orientation tomorrow then Gage drives us out day after tomorrow at daybreak. Be there on both counts."

He was gone the minute the words were out. Bethany watched him stalk down the hallway. The man still got to her. There was absolutely no denying that. It was maddening and crazy. But, maybe this was what she needed. Maybe this was the thing that would clear the air once and for all.

Nate had been living on the outskirts of her life like a larger-than-life memory. It didn't matter that he'd hurt her, the memory of him was there. She'd stalled out in the dating world—no man since had lived up to that memory…and she'd dated some really great guys. If only she'd been able to love one of them.

"Is there anyone else on the tour?" she asked, turning away and closing the door.

Amy smiled knowingly. "I know I threw you for a loop, Bethany, and I'm sorry. Do you forgive me?"

They'd been friends for a long time. "Maybe. Okay, yes. But I'm not so sure *he* will."

Amy walked around to her desk and sank into the chair that had once been Ben's. She let out a long sigh as she glanced around the office. "He'll get over it. He hasn't been the same since you left, you know."

That got Bethany. "He sent me away. Remember?"

"I remember. Still, something about the whole thing never rang true."

Bethany didn't want to dwell on her past. She'd gone over it and over it for years, and never came up with an answer. One day he'd loved her and the next he hadn't. It was as hard and as cold as that. "I survived and am a stronger woman because of what happened between us. I asked you this yesterday, but didn't get much of an answer. How are *you* surviving?"

Amy glanced out the window that had the blinds angled slightly downward, so they could see out but people couldn't see in. Bethany sank into the chair Nate had almost knocked over. Amy's weary, sad gaze came back to meet hers.

"I'm making it, Bethany. But sometimes I feel overwhelmed. Ben…" her voice rasped with emotion. She paused and drew herself up, forcing the emotion away. "He wrote me a letter basically asking me to remarry by Christmas if anything were to happen to him. Every man in the district is asking me to marry him. What was Ben thinking? Why would he ask me to do such a thing?"

It was the same question Bethany had been wondering about Amy. "He loved you and I'm sure he was thinking only the best for you."

"Yes, I know," she said, looking distant. "But even Ben can't make me fall in love with someone—he isn't an easy act to follow. How about you? Why haven't you ever married?"

Bethany shook her head, unable to admit that she felt the same way about Nate McMann. Well, it wasn't exactly the same thing. Ben James had loved Amy with his whole heart and soul. Not being able to forget a man like that was understandable. But feeling that way about a man who'd basically kicked her to the curb made her feel foolish. And she hated feeling foolish.

"I just haven't had the time to really search for the right guy. I'm sure he'll come along. But if he doesn't, I always have my work. What would we do without work?"

"I don't know. But it's my boys who

have gotten me through. I'm here at work because I have to be, but it's Dexter and Sammy who have gotten me though their daddy's death."

Bethany's heart caught with longing. "Yes, I can imagine they've been little blessings."

Amy smiled proudly. "Oh, yes. They are constant sources of joy. Their daddy would be so proud of them."

Bethany knew this was true. Ben was the kind of man who took pride in his family. He'd been a great guy.

"He'd be proud of you, too, Amy. What you are doing takes such strength."

"God has given me that. Besides, this tour company was Ben's passion. I want to help the town and also carry on his legacy. The boys may want to carry on their daddy's business one day. I want it to still be here when they are able to do that, if they choose."

"From the looks of things, you don't have anything to worry about."

Amy's brows dipped. "I don't know. The

attention from the article has helped us turn a corner economically for now, but we have to keep them coming. We can't afford to make a misstep. Every tour counts. Every positive word and great review matters. I mean, all these women are great for excitement and the attention they're bringing us, but in the long run it's the same, regular tourists who will carry this company for the future. Families like the ones on your tour."

She was absolutely right. Bethany would have to focus on that, and not on the brooding cowboy who could very easily stomp on her heart again during this tour. "I'll do my best to give this group a great experience. Now, who else is on this tour? Usually there's more than one family."

Amy took a refreshing breath and smiled excitedly. "There is. It's the cutest newlywed couple. Can you imagine wanting to take an Alaskan tour for your honeymoon? Especially one this late in the season."

It was Bethany's turn to look at Amy in horror. *"Newlyweds."*

Amy laughed. "Hold on, they've taken an Alaskan cruise here. So it's not like they got married yesterday."

"That's a relief!" Bethany exclaimed, making Amy laugh again.

"I think it's adorable, really. And since it's one of the last tours of the season and a little bit cold—they'll have plenty of snuggle time."

Bethany thought about it. "You're right, but, um, did you tell Nate about them?"

Amy looked appalled. "Are you kidding! He'll hate it if there'll be any mushy stuff going on. You should see how uptight he gets watching all this sparking and romancing that's been going on around him. It's like the guy has forgotten that love makes the world go round." A mischievous twinkle sparked in her vivid blue eyes. "I booked him *specifically* on his tour. I for one think Nate McMann needs to open his eyes and see that if he doesn't change he'll grow old alone. And it won't be pretty."

Bethany didn't know how to take that.

"I hope you don't have any ideas about me and him—"

"And what if I did?"

"Then you'd need to get rid of them right away."

"So you don't have feelings for him?"

"No, Amy, I don't. It's taken some time," she admitted. "But I don't."

Amy stood up and came around the desk. "Good. I was a bit worried that old feelings might cause problems on the tour. I'm relieved to know that won't be the case. And the sparking and romancing of the newlyweds isn't going to get to you?"

"Nope. Don't worry about me. I'll be fine." She would be fine. She *would*.

As Bethany left the building she felt relief. For a minute there, she'd feared Amy might be matchmaking. Bethany had eaten supper at Lizbet's Diner last night and had heard all about how Amy had been matchmaking over the last few months. She was more than a little relieved to know that this wasn't one of those instances.

Yes, it *had* crossed her mind the first

moment she'd walked into the room, and Nate had practically knocked his chair over bolting out of it. But then she'd found out there was a child involved, and she knew Amy wouldn't use a child.

"No, Amy, I don't have feelings for him." Bethany's words came back to her as she walked down the sidewalk. If only she could be sure those words were the truth....

Chapter Four

The Taylors were a lovely couple in their midthirties. Their son Cody was seven, extremely active and *very* curious—which Bethany thought was a good thing. It took only a few seconds after introductions were made for her to see why Shelly Taylor wasn't comfortable on the wilderness hike without help. Cody was so active that she looked one way for a second, and the next second he left the room. If that happened out on the trail he could be in danger.

Bethany had a feeling she was going to earn her keep on this trip. Especially since Nate seemed preoccupied while they loaded gear into the van. Of course, Amy had told her when she arrived that he hadn't been at all pleased to learn that Ely and Lisa March were newlyweds.

He'd learned this the day before, at the orientation meeting where they'd all met to make certain everyone had all their gear in place and understood the rules. He'd barely spoken to her, being all business— or maybe he'd thought that if he pretended she wasn't there she might just disappear. Who knew?

Nate had been cute actually—not that he would know that or that she was happy about noticing it herself. But when the two had arrived, linked together like one, Nate's thick, blond eyebrows had shot up and his eyes had narrowed. He looked over their paperwork, then glared at Amy, who smiled sweetly at him and asked him if there was anything wrong. Poor Nate, Bethany knew he wanted to say something, but he held back.

"Nothing," he replied between his gritted teeth, his gaze sliding to her. Bethany managed to keep a straight face, but she felt his pain. All evening afterwards, she'd thought about what Amy had said earlier in the week about Nate not having been the same since she'd left town. That was practically ten years ago. She wasn't about to let herself contemplate what that meant. She was certain it had nothing to do with her.

Today, as she had the day before, she continued to be distracted by him. It was as if, after being away from him for so long, that now she just couldn't get enough of looking at him. His rugged, Western jacket made his shoulders look impossibly broad, and gave her flashbacks of how protected and loved she'd once felt when he'd wrap his arms around her and hold her. She sucked in a shaky breath and told herself to remember it had all been a lie. He turned toward her at that moment and caught her looking at him. Heat rose to her cheeks, and she wanted to crawl beneath the nearest iceberg.

Hiding that need, she gave a thumbs-up signal. "I'm ready if you are. This is going to be great."

She thought his scowl was going to intensify, but instead he relaxed a touch. "You're sure you're up to this?" he asked, keeping his voice low.

Not on your life. As she stared into his indigo-blue eyes, thoughts of summer days spent hiking together beside the rivers and lakes making up this part of Alaska waylaid her. Those had been days she'd thought would never end—days that she'd wished would last forever. "I'm ready," she said feeling a quiver of uneasy longing at the memory. She would definitely have to be on her guard or she might forget that all those memories were illusions. Illusions that ended the day Nate told her he'd lied and that he didn't love her.

His gaze floated across her face. "I hope so. That little boy is going to be a handful."

"Little boys don't scare me," she said, watching Cody edging for the door once more. His dad stepped in and distracted him by teasing him. Bethany smiled watching them—determined that she was going to be upbeat about this experience. She loved watching kids with their dads. "I think it's all going to be great fun."

Bethany met Nate's gaze, and it struck her again that if they'd gotten married they would probably have had a child around Cody's age. The thought was like a splinter wedging its way into her determination to not let Nate see how much she was still affected by his rejection of her and the life they could have had together. Planting a smile on her face, she winked at him—a cover-up for the real emotions plaguing her. "I remember how much you enjoy leading tours. Even tours with rambunctious little boys. I'll never forget that set of twins that one summer. You had as much fun as they did, pulling pranks along the trail. If my memory serves me right you were the one who came out of your tent and had a bucket of water dumped on top of your head." It was true.

She laughed remembering that. "I never did know if that was Barry and Bart's doing. *Or yours.*"

He looked innocent. "I guess you'll never know."

They stared at each other for a long moment. Bethany had to keep smiling, as if that was just a cute memory between friends. It was going to be hard, but that was how she was going to approach this trip. She was fine, and no one, especially Nate, was going to know how hard this was on her.

Great fun. Nate wondered how she meant that an hour later, as they unloaded their packs from the van. He'd had them carried deep into the interior of the Chilkoot Trail. They would be hiking all day, but sleeping in a lodge for the night. It was bit of a harder trek than he normally took a family on with a small child. However, this was the way he needed to go to check out his hunch about the treasure. This was the way to Klink's Ridge and the spot where his grandfather died. Until Amy's boys had found the map hidden in a secret compartment of her kitchen cabinets, he had not understood remotely what his grandfather had been thinking. After seeing that the treasure was supposedly hidden in a spot somewhere between the Chilkoot Trail and the Taiya River, it made more sense to him. Nate was on a mission to find that spot, and maybe—just maybe—it was the same spot that X marked on the map.

He was worried about Cody, though. The little boy was active and he didn't seem to take instruction well. He hoped Bethany really was up for the hike and helping him keep up with things on the trail—Cody being number one on the priority list.

"Everyone grab your backpacks. And remember to stay close at all times. This is a tour and we are going to see the most beautiful land in the world, but it *is* wilderness. There are wild animals out there and we need to respect that—"

"Mr. McMann," Ely March cut in, tugging his new wife close to his side as he threw his paper-thin shoulders back and puffed out his chest. "It's safe though, right? They told us it was safe."

Nate hid a smile. Ely was about as big around as a pine sapling, even had a pimple on his chin, he was so young. Nineteen, but Nate was having to trust the birth date. The kid didn't look a day over sixteen. Lisa looked almost nineteen and stared at Ely like he was superman—complete adoration lighting her eyes. It was a look Nate had seen at least a dozen times over the last hour. The two kids were over the top in love and attached at the hip—how they were going to ride two horses was a mystery that was yet to be figured out.

"As long as you're aware of your surroundings and don't invade their space, they respect your space for the most part. They're much more scared of you than you are of them. But we have to remember that this is the wilderness, and that always means expect the unexpected. So let's be careful."

"Will we see bears?" Cody asked, with the great expectation of a seven-year-old. He was decked out in a red jacket, jeans and hiking boots. He had curly brown hair with big, brown eyes that saw everything, and a splash of freckles across his nose.

"We should. We'll keep watch for them."

Cody beamed. "I want to see one. I been practicin' sneakin' up on 'em."

Nate frowned and shot his parents a look that conveyed his concern. "Son, you don't sneak up on bears. I'll show you one if we come across one, but you'll see him at a good distance. We'll also see bald eagles and moose, if we get lucky."

"My mama showed me a picture of an eagle. But it wasn't bald. I'd like to see a bald one."

That got a laugh from everyone. "I'll do my best," Nate said, and then quickly explained what he was certain the boy's parents had already explained about the eagle just appearing bald with its white head.

"Did you know an eagle can spot a fish up to a mile away?" Bethany asked, coming to stand beside them.

"How far is a mile?" Cody looked up at her with an expectant expression.

"Oh, let's see," Bethany scanned the majestic countryside. "Do you see that cabin sitting down there in the valley?"

"Sure I do," Cody replied, nodding his head vigorously.

"That's about a mile."

Cody's mouth fell open and his eyes widened as he looked from the cabin to Bethany and then back to the cabin. "The eagle can see a *fish* that far away?"

"That's what the experts say. They can also fly thirty miles an hour and dive up to a hundred miles an hour."

"That's as fast as my daddy drives—"

"Whoa, son," Robert Taylor interjected, grinning. "I don't drive that fast."

"When we took mama to the hospital when she got sick you did. I saw it on the speed ohmmeter from my car seat."

Robert rubbed his jaw and grinned at Nate. "He's got me on that one. Shelly broke her arm really bad last year, and she needed to get to the hospital as fast as possible."

Shelly came up and put her arm around her husband's waist. "I'm just thankful God protected us. Poor Robert was beside himself."

"I *liked* it," Cody said. "I bet the eagle likes it, too."

Laughter rippled through the group. Nate had always enjoyed hearing Bethany laugh. It had always made him feel a deep satisfaction, and he'd never forgotten the sound of it. And nothing had changed, he still loved hearing the sound.

"It's time to get going. We're burning daylight," he said, a bit rougher than he'd meant, but he didn't need to be standing around beside Bethany, reminiscing about the good old days and what could have been. It was too dangerous. He had to survive five days out here on this trail, and getting all sentimental wasn't going to help him at all.

Ely helped Lisa get her backpack on and she rewarded him with a kiss just as Nate walked past them. He immediately remembered kissing Bethany out here in

God's country—memories were going to be everywhere. Behind him Bethany chuckled at something someone said and his heart squeezed tight—he wasn't going to be able to get away from her and the memories this entire trip. He quickened his steps, grabbed his backpack and hit the trail.

This was going to be a long day—and a long, long week.

And one he knew, without a doubt, he was going to regret.

The wilderness hadn't changed. Bethany was bringing up the rear of the tour and enjoying the beauty around her. Neither the Marches nor the Taylors had wanted a history lesson over the Chilkoot Trail. They'd simply wanted to see some of Alaska's wilderness. The passage they were hiking today was one she remembered well. The hike was uphill most of the way, but there were no cliffs to worry about Cody falling from, and yet there were spots where you could look out across the valley that was surrounded by snowcapped mountains. It would absolutely take your breath away.

The only problem for Bethany was that she kept getting distracted from the scenery because she kept watching both families with wistful thoughts pounding away at her. The newlyweds held hands, kissed and encouraged each other to the point of it being sappy. Bethany thought they were darling, being so in love. The sweetness of that new love was touching—in her business, she was around young love all the time, and it made her wistful. If only things had been different…she'd had to learn to live with her own disappointment and not let it affect her livelihood. It was odd, really, how she could live with a broken heart but still enjoy weddings for others.

She had just pushed everything aside and had not dwelled on it. That had been the best way for her to deal with it—once she'd realized that she had to move forward.

But being on this trip with Nate right there in front of her, leading this tour like all those years ago, when she'd believed he loved her, made it all come rushing back.

Watching Ely and Lisa and the lovely,

more mature, loving relationship between Robert and Shelly Taylor had her longing for what should have been.

"I want to see a bear. A big bear," Cody informed them, when they stopped to rest a couple of hours later.

"We see them often on this trail," Nate said. "But it will be further along and from a distance. There's a great bear-viewing spot that we call Hunch Hill Overlook," Nate said, meeting her gaze. He was tense.

Bethany knew the spot well, they themselves named it that, for the odd look of the mountain and cropping across the way. "It's a great place. Everyone eat a granola bar and take a break," she said, encouraging them and moving to stand beside Nate while everyone headed to some fallen tree trunks to sit.

She hoped when they saw bears that Cody didn't try to scale the mountain to reach the animals. He'd made several sudden dashes into the woods when he saw a scurrying rabbit or other startled animal taking shelter. Cody's dad had patiently taken off after him and brought him back. She was just glad that most animals were heading in the opposite direction from them and that none of them took offense at being chased. The little boy had a thing about running off—it was as if he thought it was a game. Bethany was worn out just watching him, and she could tell Nate was tense.

"Loosen up," she said.

He grunted. "I've never seen a kid run off so much. It could be a problem. He's like a jumping jellybean."

No sooner than he'd spoken than Cody began jumping and pointing toward the woods. "A bear!"

"Where? Where?" Ely yelled, hopping in front of Lisa, arms out as if ready to do hand-to-hand combat.

Bethany automatically moved between Cody and the woods and Nate did the same, as everyone scanned the area.

"I don't see him." Nate looked at Cody. "Did you get a good look at him?"

Bethany had her doubts about whether

Cody had actually seen a bear or if he'd wanted to see one so badly that he'd imagined it. Nate probably had the same thought but would never let Cody know he doubted him. She liked that about Nate…he would have made such a great daddy. The idea ambushed her, twisting her heart like a dishrag.

"I saw him good. I'm gonna go find that ole bear," Cody said, puffing out his seven-year-old chest and heading toward the woods.

"Oh no you're not, young man." Shelly grabbed him by the back of the jacket and halted him.

"Are we in danger?" Ely wrapped his arm around Lisa, who was glancing around nervously. He was becoming a broken record.

Nate pushed his Stetson off his forehead, his blue eyes serious but conveying trust and security as he looked at the group. "As we explained in orientation, there are always risks involved in a wilderness tour, but I've never had any trouble with bears and I've been leading tours since I was in high school."

Relief eased the tension of Lisa's expression, as she looked up at Ely. "It's okay, sweetie. I'm not afraid. Mr. McMann knows what he's doing."

A cold gust of wind blew through and Ely pushed a dancing wisp of hair out of her eyes. His expression was absolute adoration. "Even if he didn't, I wouldn't let anything happen to you."

Lisa melted right there in front of everyone. "I know you wouldn't."

Bethany melted herself. What woman wouldn't want to hear that from the man she loved?

"I'm going to check for signs," Nate growled in her ear, startling her. "We start the second leg of the hike in fifteen minutes. Watch him," he snapped, nodding toward Cody.

Bethany sucked in a cold breath of air and watched Nate stalk off into the woods. The temperature had been hovering around fifty degrees, but it suddenly felt like fifty below. What had just gotten into Nate?

There was so much about Nate McMann that she'd loved…but he'd broken things off. Watching him go now sent a chill to her bones, reminding her of that day ten years ago.

Turning away, she forced a smile as she faced her group. "We have fifteen minutes. I suggest we sit on those rocks and relax and enjoy this beautiful spot. Nate is scouting around, and if there is anything out there that might want to do us harm he'll scare it off."

She led the way to the rather large boulders sitting at the base of a sloping hill. Ely and Lisa immediately sat off to the side by themselves. Lisa leaned back against Ely, and he draped his arms about her as they stared out across the horizon at the snow-covered mountains. Bethany eased her backpack from her back and had to smile as Cody scampered over and did as she did. When she sat her pack down at the base of a rock, he sat his carefully beside hers before climbing up on the rock beside her. His cheeks were a touch pink from the wind and Bethany's heartstrings were tugged just looking at him.

"Are you having fun?" She pulled two protein bars from her pocket and handed him one.

"Yes ma'am. I'm gonna like the horses the best, though. When do we ride them?"

"Tomorrow and the day after is when we ride. Have you ever ridden a horse before?"

He nodded. "I rode a pony at the fair last year." He frowned. "But this man walked beside the horse and we only rode in a circle."

His disgust was thick in his voice, making her hide a chuckle. Out of the corner of her eye Bethany saw Robert reach for Shelly's hand. They smiled at each other then looked back at Cody. Clearly, they loved their little boy.

"I can certainly see where that would bother you."

"Oh, yeah, I'm seven now, I don't need nobody holding my horse."

"Well, I can understand that, also. But you know, there are rules out here in the Alaskan wilderness. Our tour company is pretty strict when it comes to kids. Your horse will have to be tied to me. But the good news is we won't be going in circles inside a fence. Is that going to bother you too much?"

He sighed a heavy sigh. "I guess not, but one day I'm gonna be able to do things myself."

She laughed. "That day will get here before you know it." She reached out and gave him a hug. "We're going to have fun tomorrow. I promise."

Glancing around, she took a deep breath herself and tried to focus only on what was happening now. Not on the past. Not on the fact that she was sitting here alone when she should have had a family of her own by now. Time flew. It marched forward and disappeared behind her quicker than she could ever believed.

She was sitting in this beautiful place God had created, and she felt suddenly alone—it wasn't as if she hadn't felt that way before. Ever since Nate broke up with her all those years ago, she'd felt that way, but she'd managed to push those feelings away for the most part and get on with her life. But she'd felt distant from God, too. And the gulf she felt, the abandonment and aloneness she felt was because God had done nothing to ease the pain of what had happened to her.

"I will never leave you or forsake you"—the verse came to her clearly, as if God spoke it out loud on the breeze. Bethany tugged her turtleneck higher about her chin and blinked against the sudden sting of tears. God might have said that promise, but it wasn't true.

God had left her high and dry. Alone. Just like Nate had.

Chapter Five

Nate stormed through the trees, putting as much distance between him and Bethany as possible. It wasn't bad enough that he had to be paired with her on this five-day tour, but he had to be paired with two couples who clearly loved each other and weren't afraid to show it!

The kissing and hugging, and the blasted sugar was flowing so freely it was enough to drive him crazy. And the look on Bethany's face—the longing was clearly there. She'd even *sighed* when Ely gushed all that stuff out just now.

How was he supposed to keep his mind off thoughts of Bethany—how she'd felt in his arms and how much fun they'd had? He was struggling. He still loved her. That hadn't changed.

And he knew it never would.

But she could not know that. The last thing he needed was for her to know that all he could think about a few minutes ago was kissing her. It had been almost ten years since he'd felt his lips against hers. Frustration ate at him. It had been almost ten years since he'd heard her whisper how much she loved him, and he could still hear her sweet voice, as clear now as then.

It had been almost ten years since his world had been right and since he'd had every blessing a man could have.

Almost ten years since God had stopped smiling down on him. *Focus man, focus. You have a job to do.*

He did, and he knew it. He would give this group their money's worth on this tour, and also seek the treasure that might help Treasure Creek get back up on its feet again. That was his job.

Breathing hard from thrashing through

the underbrush, he halted. Shrugging out of his backpack, he set it on the ground, bent on one knee and unzipped the front pocket. He pulled out the folded piece of paper that Amy had given him earlier that morning. It was a copy of the original treasure map.

The map was misleading in many ways. There were no specifics. It was like trying to find a needle in a haystack. It was going to take everyone searching for the treasure to find it, because the map covered such a huge expanse of wilderness. Even with the tour guides of the Alaska's Treasures tour company looking for it, locating the spot was going to be tough. There wasn't any other group of people who were more familiar with the wilderness on the map than them. So far, there hadn't been much luck, but there had been some unwanted attention that made him worry about the safety of Amy and anyone else who might be in contact with the map. Looking at it, he couldn't help but wonder if everyone who carried it was being watched? He glanced around through the trees, his gaze quickly noting every detail. There was no one watching him—and there was also no bear or sign that a bear had been around. Calmer, he stood. Night would be here soon. It was time to go back.They had a cabin to reach before that happened.

He folded the map and placed it inside his backpack. There was nothing about this area that hinted at anything familiar on the map. The cabin three days away was the place he was interested in. He shifted from one boot to the other, and his mind shifted straight back to Bethany and her reason for being here.

Despite her bluster, he had a feeling she hadn't hiked in a decade. She'd been too busy. He'd kept up with her through the years and been proud that she'd made her dreams come true. And that was what he didn't understand. She'd done weddings in Italy, France and other places he'd never had any desire to travel to, but that she'd dreamed of. So why had she come back to Treasure Creek? And how soon would it be before she left again?

He'd let her go once…he wasn't sure if he could do it again. Not without at least seeing if she'd have him. But that wasn't fair to her. Spinning on his boot, he headed back toward camp, feeling about as low as a man could feel. He knew there was no way he'd ever expose his heart or his secret to Bethany. He was going to have to just get over it, and that was that.

All in all, the first day's hike took longer than expected, but everyone took some awesome photos. And of course, Lisa and Ely got in a few more kisses before they walked into the camp clearing.

Bethany could tell it was bothering Nate.

She saw it in the way he held his shoulders so stiffly as he marched onward. Yes, all the giggles were getting to him—at least that was what she suspected was getting to him. She thought the couple was cute, but it sure did make her think about things she'd be far better off not thinking about…like kissing Nate. And being alone—but she'd given herself a good talking to after having her little pity party out there earlier.

"I think the first day went well," she said, later that evening, after they'd gotten camp ready for the night. She was trying for a decent conversation with Nate. They were standing on the outer edge of the campfire's glow, away from everyone. Darkness had just fallen when they'd finally reached the rustic four-room cabin that would be their lodging for the night. The men bunked in one room, and the women in another. The newlyweds were having separation issues and had cuddled up on one side of the fire like two peas in a pod.

Nate was glowering again. He stood with arms crossed, his hat pulled down low over his eyes and a big frown on his face. He grunted instead of answering, and in the firelight she saw his eyes shoot toward the couple who were in between kisses and gazing starry-eyed up at the big, expansive sky.

She'd meant that last comment to get at least a smile, or even a grunt of humor. But no. "You know, you're going to have to be a bit nicer, or you're going to give Amy's tour company a bad name," she added, only half joking.

He shot her a glare. "I didn't know until yesterday that I had a newlywed couple on this tour. How am I supposed to be happy about that? They've hardly looked at the scenery. It's wasted on them."

Bethany laughed. "So? What's wrong with seeing two people in love? Or do you just have something against love?" Maybe she shouldn't have said that, but the man was being a complete jerk. Yes, sometimes the newlyweds' kissing was a bit uncomfortable, but only because she was hiking with Nate.

"This is a family tour." He wasn't giving up.

"Shelly thinks they're sweet."

"I hope they know they won't be able to live in the real world and not be separated at longer intervals than fifteen minutes. Look at them."

"It's a *campfire*, Nate. Or don't you

remember?" Oh, now she'd gone and done it! Opened her big mouth and stuck her foot straight in, sideways. And instead of stopping, she just kept on going. "You don't have any right to judge them," she finished, doing some glowering of her own.

He was quiet on that note. They both stared at the fire in uncomfortable silence. She didn't know for certain what he was thinking, but *she* was thinking about all the campfires *they'd* watched burn together... all the cuddling they'd done.

"We hit a harder area tomorrow," he said, finally. "You're going to have to keep a stricter eye on Cody when we stop along the trail. I don't want him wandering off. Seriously, with all the notice we've gotten from the magazine article, the last thing we need is the bad publicity having lost a child out here would bring."

Bethany tensed at his words. "For your information, I *have* been watching him. So have his parents. Where have you been?" she snapped. "You don't need to worry about Cody. Do you not think I know how to do my job?" Okay, so that wasn't exactly what she'd meant to say. But really, did the man think she was incompetent?

"I didn't say that."

"It sounded pretty close to that."

They glared at each other, both knowing this had more to do with their past than this moment. Years of anger rioted inside of Bethany, suddenly fighting for exposure and release. Her gaze dropped to his mouth—a hard, grim line. It hurt to remember how he'd once smiled so easily at her. Why had she come on this trip? She should have backed out the instant she found out it was going to be with Nate.

"Fine," Nate grunted. "Hear what you want to hear, just watch the boy."

Argggg! Bethany wanted to scream. So much for conversation. That had been a bust from every angle.

She had a good mind to follow him and give him a big piece of her mind. But she didn't. What good would it do?

This was just their first day. Better to let it slide and hope tomorrow was better.

* * *

She was driving him crazy. Nate stopped behind the cabin where the firewood was stacked. It was the second time that day that he'd walked away from Bethany. It was the only way to keep himself out of trouble. When her green eyes flashed like emerald flames, he'd wanted to kiss her. Not because she was so angry, but because all he'd seen was the pain in her eyes when he'd told her he didn't love her. That pain had caused him more hurt than she would ever know.

She'd shown him tonight that her spunk was still alive and well and that he hadn't killed that wonderful part of her.

But he was goading her to keep his feelings at bay. It wasn't a good thing.

He snatched his hat from his head and rammed uneasy fingers through his hair. Bethany had always been alive and full of life. He'd loved that about her. He liked knowing she was still the same Bethany.

Settling his hat back on his head he grabbed up an armful of logs for the fireplace, and headed back around the cabin to put the wood inside. He was going to have to improve his attitude.

Just rounding the corner he was startled to see Bethany standing at the far end of the cabin from him. She was leaning against the small building, out of the view of the campers—with her head in her hands. Her shoulders heaved once, as if she was taking a deep breath.

She looked so alone.

As alone as he felt. He hated that.

His heart clenched. He was hurting her again… It took every ounce of willpower to not go to her. But he couldn't do that. He had to make it through this and then let her go.

Taking a quiet step backwards, he edged around the corner of the cabin, flattening himself against the rough logs. Leaning his head back, he stared up at the sky, feeling like a number-one loser.

Out here, God was everywhere. A man couldn't come to the wilds of Alaska and not know that God was real. He was a tangible presence in this vast, untamed territory, as undeniable as the beauty that surrounded them. And yet, Nate felt as far away from God as he could possibly get.

He leaned around and peeked at Bethany again, unable to get the picture of her with her head in her hands out of his mind. He'd badgered her into feeling bad. It was his fault she was standing there like that, hiding.

"Hey there, Mr. Nate! Whatcha doin'?"

Nate shot away from the building, so startled by the surprise appearance of Cody that he dropped the wood he was carrying. "Cody! What are you doing back here?" he asked, keeping his voice low. Hurriedly, he knelt and started scooping up the wood. Talk about getting caught—the last thing he wanted was for Bethany to realize he was back here and had seen her.

She might think he was spying on her or something. Boy, that wouldn't be good.

"I'm lookin' for horses. My dad says we're ridin' 'em tomorrow, but I can't find 'em nowhere. You seen any?"

"They're being brought in first thing in

the morning. Look, Cody, your mamma is going to be looking for you. You don't need to be going off by yourself."

"What's going on?"

Too late, Nate slowly turned his head and looked up at Bethany as he picked up the last log. Of course, Cody was all too willing to answer her question.

"I come lookin' for horses and found Mr. Nate lookin' at you," he said proudly. "I scared him."

Nate groaned inwardly as he rose up, forced his shoulders back and met Bethany's knowing gaze. If it hadn't been for the slight sliver of light reaching them from a window in the cabin, he wouldn't have been able to see the way she'd hiked her brow at him.

"He was *watching* me?"

"Yup, I come up behind him and looked around to see if he was lookin' at horses, but it was only you down there."

Talk about being thrown from a bull and trampled—Nate was getting tromped on worse than by a two-thousand-pound killer—by an eight-year-old!

"I wasn't—"

"Cody," Bethany said, cutting Nate off and reaching for Cody's hand. "Sweetie, you can't go wandering around in the dark by yourself. Come on, let's go find your mother before she misses you."

Speaking of which, where was his mom? Nate started to say something. The kid wasn't being watched as closely as needed—just like Bethany had accused him of saying earlier.

She cut warning eyes at him and realized she was thinking the same thing. "Don't say a word. Not one word. He *is* being watched." She hissed the last part.

That said, she marched off with Cody in tow. She was totally not happy that Cody had gotten away from her again. Nate watched her disappear around the corner, and for the first time since she'd come to town, he felt a smile crack across his face.

She was just as cute being mad at twenty-nine as she'd been when she was nineteen.

Chapter Six

The cabin had been stocked with fresh eggs, bacon and biscuit mix to enable the guests to have a hearty breakfast. Bethany woke early to the soft beeping of her alarm so that she could help prepare it. She hadn't hiked much in a very long time and she'd fallen asleep from exhaustion the moment her head hit the pillow. She was glad she could move without hurting too much.

Just as she'd assumed, Nate was up when she entered the main room. He glanced up from adding a log to the wood stove. "Good morning."

The man shouldn't look so wonderful at five-thirty in the morning. It was a crime, that's what it was. *She* probably looked like roadkill, while he looked like the poster boy for the *Now Woman* magazine article, with his five o'clock shadow and piercing blue eyes. The man was incredibly handsome, but standing there in his red flannel shirt and jeans—okay, whoa, it was not good for her to continually think about him like this.

"Are you okay this morning?" he asked. "Not still mad at me?"

She expected it. "No. I'm fine. Cody is fine, and I'll make sure to keep watch over him today. He is quick. Shelly said he was there and then he was gone. She was really sorry he got away from her like that."

"Kids get away fast. You and I both know that from previous tours. I'm not trying to be unreasonable."

"I know that," she said, knowing as well as he did that there was much more going on between them than what was being said. Yes, Cody's safety was a major concern, but this wasn't just about Cody. Looking away, she walked to the small kitchen counter and grabbed the biscuit mix, fighting the urge to ask him if he'd really been spying on her last night. According to Cody, he'd been watching her around the corner. When he stalked off she was so mad she'd needed a minute to herself. He'd gone into the woods, on the other side of the cabin. At least she thought he had, and that was why she'd chosen the far side of the cabin to take a few minutes alone. She didn't expect him to see her.

He came and stood beside her as she began preparing the biscuit mix. His arm brushed hers when he reached for the large skillet and the bacon. They had this routine down. They'd done many breakfast for their tours together and they fell back into their routine like it had been yesterday.

"I wasn't sure you'd remember about the breakfast, since I didn't mention it."

She paused from mixing the biscuits and looked up at him. "I remember." She took a breath and refocused on the biscuits. Beside her, Nate was silent, but she could feel his gaze on her as she dumped the biscuit dough onto the counter and reached for the rolling pin. Her arm brushed his again and that aggravatingly, wonderful electrical shock wave of awareness sizzled through her—not good. Not good.

"Yeah, me, too," he said, turning to the stove, where he began frying the bacon in the skillet he'd been heating.

There wasn't anything Bethany had forgotten about their time together. She'd tried, but Nate had become a larger-than-life figure in her memory, and it was hard to wipe an image like that away. No man had ever stood a chance, going up against his memory...even after the heartache he'd caused her.

These five days with him should help that.

Surely, by the time they were done she wouldn't have this overblown image of him blocking her good sense. She'd remember all the not so good things about him. Surely, at twenty-nine she could see clearly. Starting now...with getting her thoughts back on track with this trip, and not on the man standing beside her.

"Is there anything I need to know about today?" she asked, moving slightly, so that there was no chance of her arm brushing his again. This was business.

"The horses will be arriving in about an hour. Royce is bringing them over from the ranch."

"How is Royce?" She'd always loved Nate's ranch foreman and his wife. "And Sue, how is she?"

"They're doing well. Royce keeps threatening to retire, but Sue just laughs and tells him to stop fibbing."

Bethany smiled as she plopped the cut-out biscuits into the skillet. "I always loved those two."

"They loved you, too."

Bethany couldn't stop herself. She looked at him hard. He turned instantly back to his frying bacon. "The biscuits are ready for the oven," she said, holding down the flare of anger.

She wouldn't do that. She wouldn't go

there. Today it was about being reasonable and getting along. It wasn't about the past.

As if summoned, in that moment lights cut across the dark windows of the cabin and the low growl of a truck filled the air. "Looks like Royce is running early," Nate said, lifting bacon from the pan with a fork and placing it on a paper towel-covered plate.

"I'll let him in."

Bethany hurried to the door and opened it just a crack, not wanting to let the cold air into the warm cabin as she waited for the lanky cowboy. Royce hopped from the cab of the Dodge and ambled her way. She widened the crack just as he stepped up onto the small porch and grinned widely.

"Bethany Marlow, you are a sight for sore eyes." He grabbed her up in a hug.

"Same to you, too, Royce." She hugged him tight.

"Me and Sue couldn't believe it when we heard you were coming home," he said, then softly into her ear. "It's about time." He gave her one last squeeze before stepping back. "Smells like you've got things cooking, Nate."

"We're working on it. Bethany made the biscuits."

"Just like Sue taught me."

"You'll need to come out to the ranch and see Sue. She can't wait to see you."

"I will. I promise."

"Well, while y'all finish up here I'll go get the horses out of the trailer. I brought Freckles, like you said, and he's feeling frisky knowing he's going on the trail."

Bethany laid a hand over her heart. "He's still alive and well?"

Royce gave a mock look of shock. "That horse is gonna outlive us all. There's not another one around any better to put a child on, either."

"I know. Never was." Bethany knew Cody would be safe on Freckles. He was the sweetest-tempered horse she'd ever been on. "Cody will be so excited."

"Good. Well, I'll get to it. Talk to you in a bit, young lady." He paused at the door, put his hands on his hips and grinned at her. "It is really great to have you home."

"Can I get on him?" Cody had been a ball of excitement ever since breakfast, when he looked out the window to find horses lined up and saddled.

"Not yet," his dad, Robert, told him once again.

Robert was so patient with Cody, and it was easy to see that the two loved each other very much. Bethany found herself watching them and also Shelly. Shelly watched her husband and son, too, with an adoring look lighting her face. Then she stepped up and wrapped her arm around Robert's waist and leaned her head against his shoulder. "You're sure he's going to be safe on the horse?"

Nate was busy finishing up closing down the camp, so the question was directed to Bethany. She felt confident with answering it, since she was so familiar with Freckles. "You couldn't ask for a better horse than Freckles. He knows the trails and has the temperament of a church mouse. I'll also be riding beside him with a lead rope. And the trail is easy. Nate's chosen a very safe trail around the lake. He'll enjoy it."

"He'll be fine," Robert said.

"And if he gets scared or uncomfortable, I'll take him on the horse with me," Bethany added. "I've done that on many tours."

"I can ride my own horse," Cody said. "I ain't afraid."

"*Not* afraid, don't say *ain't*," Shelly corrected.

"Yes, ma'am, but I ain't afraid."

Within the next few minutes they got everyone situated. Nate rode in front, Ely and Lisa followed him, then Shelly. Robert and Bethany and Cody brought up the rear. Once again, Cody talked nonstop. Bethany had the most wonderful time. She told him about the bears he was so interested in, and how they didn't come up and bother hikers too much unless food was left out. They talked about how to keep food away from them, and he was enthralled when he found out that they hung it on poles so that the bears couldn't reach it.

Bethany felt her heartstrings tug—she wanted children. Always had, but without a husband in sight that dream was hard to come by. Lately, it had been on her mind more and more. She'd even toyed a time or two with the idea of adopting on her own. But raising a child without a husband was—well, it was scary. And it just wasn't how she'd envisioned her life. She'd want a family, the whole package. But she thought, smiling at Cody, if that wasn't possible she just might have to think more seriously about her options.

"I want to see a bear," Cody said, after a while.

Bethany could only chuckle. He was a broken record. She really hoped that before the trip was over Cody got to see his bear.

There were many things about riding on horseback that Bethany enjoyed. One, simply the fact that she was riding again, and two, being on horseback kept Ely and Lisa a little separated. She had to admit that watching them snuggle and be so lovey-dovey was getting to her.

Nate filled the silence with a lot of stories about the people who'd traversed the Chilkoot Trail. Even though they weren't following the actual trail, he still gave some history on the many people who'd made the treacherous journey in the expectation of striking it rich in the gold fields of the Klondike. As many times as she'd heard Nate relate the information, she always loved hearing him share.

His very own ancestor, at the age of nineteen, had made nearly ten trips across the pass, carrying the supplies required to last him a year. He didn't strike it rich, but he managed to sift enough gold from his stake to come back to Treasure Creek and buy the land that Nate ranched today.

It was a neat story, and all the time she was dating Nate she'd known that he would never leave Treasure Creek. The land was in his blood. How she'd thought they would have a life together back then, when she'd known she was leaving, was still a mystery to her. But Nate had solved that problem for her.

They stopped for lunch on a knoll overlooking a beautiful valley. The forty-something temperature didn't seem to bother anyone.

"So you've been leading these tours since you were in high school?" Robert asked Nate, as they sat around a small campfire that Nate had started.

"Yeah, I started it when Ben opened the company and needed guides. I had lived here most of my life and loved ranching, but I was looking for a little adventure." He smiled, and Bethany's heart did a lunging dive.

"Alaska looks like the place for adventure," Ely said. "We really enjoyed our cruise. I was teasing Lisa and told her I was going to get a job and move here."

"I told him it's pretty, but I don't want to be here in the really cold weather."

Nate looked at Bethany. "You get used to it."

She couldn't help adding. "You actually miss the different seasons when you leave."

Nate's brows dipped in the shadow of his Stetson. "That surprises me," he said. "I thought you couldn't wait to get to warmer weather."

She shrugged. "Sometimes it takes leaving to realize what you miss." She really wished she hadn't said that, but it was the truth. He could take it as he wanted.

"When are we gonna ride horses again?" Cody asked, busy eating a protein bar. He'd turned his back on the group and was sitting so he could watch the horses. He was enthralled with animals.

"We're about to hop back on them as soon as we clean up camp," Nate said. "Do you want to help me put out the fire?"

Cody sprang up from the log. "Sure I do."

Everyone laughed and stood up. Bethany was more than glad to have the distraction. She hadn't known what to think about Nate's comments. Had he thought she didn't like it here in Alaska? Had she given him that impression? Probably, since she'd only ever talked about getting away and traveling. He had every reason to be totally confused by her.

She had been wanting him and her career *and* children. She was still confused even now.

Within minutes, they were all mounting their horses again. Nate seemed distant once more, as if what she'd said had affected him. The tension between them was like hot-and-cold water. There was just no getting around that they were having trouble being around each other. It was like walking on eggshells.

There was so much she wanted to say to him and so many questions she wanted answered, and yet she couldn't ask. It was embarrassing. With each passing minute, she knew she wanted answers. Needed answers.

Deserved answers.

Several times along the trail that afternoon, Nate signaled for Bethany to take the lead, and he detoured into the woods.

There were no signs along the trail connected to anything on the map. But he still felt that the last cabin on the trail was his best bet. The cabins had been maintained over the years by different people. Some had been redone by the tour company, but they remained basically historic properties. Given that everyone knew there was supposed to be a secret tunnel in one cabin, it only made sense that this could be what his grandfather Chester thought he'd found. And maybe Mack Tanner had actually found it. Who knew? This cabin near the cliff might have a tunnel leading to it from the crevice to the cabin. He was going to climb down and explore it.

He tried to concentrate on the landscape, but his mind had focused on Bethany. She'd insinuated that she missed Treasure Creek. Had she gone away and realized this was where she should be? His heart felt as if an iron stake had just been shot through it. How was he going to live near her every day if she stayed? All this time, he'd been making it by thinking she would be leaving. But what if she stayed?

When she walked into the kitchen that morning, she'd taken his breath away. She was everything he'd ever wanted. He loved the way her eyes lit when she spoke. Loved the way her dark hair swung when she walked toward him.

He remembered morning hugs and kisses when they'd been on tours together. They'd had as much trouble saying good night as Ely and Lisa were having, except they had to be more professional about it, since they were leading the tours. It was tolerable because they'd planned to get married that summer, and the dynamics of their time together would have changed. They'd have been husband and wife and he would have been able to love her and hold her all he wanted.

He was following a trail that ran parallel to the trail Bethany was on with the group, and the sunlight was filtering in through the dense trees. Every once in a while the sound of the groups' laughter would drift to him, and he wondered what they were laughing at. Probably something Bethany had said. She was a funny person—or she had been. Maybe when he wasn't around she still was.

The tension between them was so tight that they were both having trouble functioning. Pausing his horse in a beam of sunlight, he stared up at Heaven again. It seemed he'd been looking for God's guidance more in the last couple of days than he had in years. His anger at God was still there. But he hadn't let that anger eat him alive. He had to come to terms with it, and he'd settled on indifference. God had been indifferent to him, and so he'd been indifferent to God. But now there was that small voice inside of him saying that maybe this time God might hear him. That this time God might decide to throw him a lifeline. Only, what could that lifeline be? He couldn't have children. There was no medical way that he could.

He'd had multiple second opinions on his condition, but the results were all the same. He couldn't father children. And Bethany had said once that she wasn't comfortable with adoption. That being the case, there was nothing for them.

Hanging his head, Nate found himself praying. It felt odd, rusty, as he asked God to hear him. It felt like he shouldn't ask, because he had been away so long…but he asked anyway. "Maybe You have a plan I don't know about," he said. "Maybe bringing Bethany home is part of that plan and it involves me." He paused, the words sticking in his throat. "And maybe nothing about her involves me, and I have to get used to that all over again. But whatever the plan is, Lord, I pray that You give me some kind of closure. I can't do this on my own. I've been trying, but one look at her and I know I'm going to mess everything up if I don't find a way to hold my feelings inside. I can't have her look at me with pity in those beautiful green eyes of hers. I'm asking You to give me strength, Lord."

Just as he opened his eyes a scream pierced the quiet.

Chapter Seven

Every horrible scenario Nate could think of flashed through his mind as he sent Clyde, his horse, racing through the trees toward Bethany and the group. His heart thundered in his chest, drowning out the thunder of Clyde's hooves.

He leaned low as Clyde ducked under limbs and hurdled fallen trunks with the expertise of a horse well adapted to his surroundings. Nate almost ran into a black bear as it stormed across his path, heading deep into the woods. Obviously, there had been an encounter of some sort. He hoped the scream he'd heard had simply been from fright at seeing the bear up close, and nothing more serious. He made it to the trail, and Clyde followed it over a ridge. Just over the top, he brought the big bay to a skidding halt. The group had all dismounted and Bethany was kneeling over Lisa.

Nate threw himself from the saddle before Clyde stopped. "What happened?"

"It was a *bear!* A real, live *bear,*" Cody exclaimed. "It stood up and scared Lisa's horse. She fell *right off.*"

Bethany was beside her, examining Lisa's foot, while Ely held her hand.

"I'm fine," Lisa said. "Really."

Bethany looked at Nate as he knelt down beside her. "She seems fine. She said she didn't land hard. The ground is pretty soft right here. But I want to be sure before I let her up."

"Yeah," Ely said. "Me, too."

Nate held the young woman's chin in his hand and checked her pupils. "Your eyes look fine. You didn't hit your head?"

"No. I just slid off like I was going down a slide. I screamed from fright, not pain."

Nate grinned at the look of embarrassment in her expression. "You look fine to me. And don't be embarrassed. I saw your bear hightailing it back toward Canada. I think you scared him just as much as he scared you."

She laughed. "Probably so, with the scream. But really, I've never seen a bear that close. He just reared up out of nowhere."

"I was terrified, too, if that helps," Shelly said, leaning down to give her a hug. "I hate to say it, but Cody saw his bear at your expense. Are you sure you don't hurt anywhere?"

"I might be a little sore tomorrow, but really, everyone, I'm fine."

Robert was studying her as hard as Nate. "She was lucky, from what I saw."

"Yeah, 'cause it was a giant bear," Cody said, spinning around, staring out into the woods. "It's a wonder it didn't try to eat her."

As usual, his comment made everyone laugh. "Why y'all laughing," he asked indignantly. "It could'a ate her in *two* bites."

Nate had heard enough. He took her arm. "If you're game, let's get you up. Ely, you ready?"

Ely nodded and took her other arm. "If Lisa is I am. She's a tough cookie," he said, grinning at her. She blinked doe eyes at him, as if he'd just told her she was the most beautiful woman in all the world. Nate met Bethany's concerned gaze and felt his heart squeeze. "We'll just watch her closely at camp tonight."

Bethany nodded and touched his biceps. "Okay," she said, but he could see in her eyes, and the way she squeezed his arm, that she'd been shaken and was hiding it from the group.

He and Ely got Lisa standing and she chuckled. "See? I'm as good as it gets. No broken bones or anything. I'm even going to get back on that horse and dare that bear to come back and try to knock me off again. It's not happening."

Nate grinned. "You're tougher than you look."

Ely hugged her. "What'd I tell you? That's my girl."

Nate went to get her horse. He motioned for Bethany to come with him. He wanted to make sure the horse wasn't still spooked, and he wanted to make sure Bethany was okay.

He took the reins of Starlight, the horse Lisa had been riding, and led the mare down the path away from everyone. Bethany walked beside him silently, as if she knew what he was doing. They'd walked about thirty feet, when the trail bent to the right around the woods. "Are you alright?" he asked, halting.

She looked pale. "That scared me. She slid right off Starlight. Nate, that horse was so scared by that bear, it reared so high it almost toppled backwards. That's why she didn't hit hard, Starlight's rear was so close to the ground Lisa didn't have far to drop. She just didn't realize that her horse almost fell on top of her. All I could think about was her being hurt really bad—" her voice broke.

"It's okay," Nate said, draping his arm about Bethany's shoulders before he thought better of what he was doing. It was just as natural a thing for him to do as breathing—pulling the woman he loved close to comfort her when she was distressed. She stepped close instantly, her forehead resting in the crook of his neck. She felt so wonderful in his arms, so perfect.

"You looked like you had it under control when I came up on you," he managed, breathing in the scent of her, while fighting his emotions. He closed his eyes, feeling weaker in that moment than he'd felt in years. He never thought he'd be holding Bethany again. It was a very dangerous thing for him. When her arms went around him and she leaned her head back their eyes met and he couldn't think straight. He swallowed hard, his heart pounded—and he almost dipped his lips to hers before coming to his senses. Gently, he let her go and stepped back. "We need to get going," he said. "If you're okay."

"I'm fine. Great," she said. "Thanks for the support."

He nodded, knowing she knew what he'd been thinking. It was a wonder she hadn't slapped him for it.

"You go ahead. I'll bring the horse in a minute."

"Sure," she said, walking away as she spoke. Feeling like a jerk, he watched her go. He shouldn't have crossed that line. He shouldn't have touched her.

Letting Amy rope him into this reunion on the trail had been the worst mistake he'd made in years.

He'd almost kissed her! And worse, she would have let him. Bethany was so humiliated she couldn't stand it. If he hadn't chosen to abort the idea, she would have been lip-locked with the man.

Embarrassed, she'd spent the rest of the afternoon trying hard to conceal the con-voluted emotions racing through her. Nate had pulled her into his arms and she'd gone willingly. Like a moth to a flame. It was pathetic!

They'd stopped now, to let the guys fish and also to give Lisa some time out of the saddle. Bethany and Shelly had opted to sit with her on a blanket and watch.

"Are you hurting?" Bethany asked her, as she eased down onto the blanket.

"My hip is a bit tender, but I'm good. And this feels great."

"Oh, yeah, and it's beautiful, too," Shelly cooed, stretching out her legs and leaning back on her elbows.

Bethany watched Nate getting the guys situated with their poles.

"So what's the story between you and our fearless leader?"

The question from Shelly caught Bethany off guard, and she realized she was staring at Nate. She pulled a bag of trail mix from her backpack. "What do you mean?"

"I know what she means." Lisa gave a knowing smile. "Everybody should, with the way you two keep giving each other those smokin' hot looks."

Bethany almost choked on her trail mix. "I haven't given him a look like that. And *he* certainly hasn't given me one." Had she? Had *he? Mad looks, maybe.*

Lisa and Shelly laughed.

"Yeah, right," Shelly drawled. "So what's the story? We're out here in the boonies, so we can't help but be nosey. Are y'all dating and have had a fight? Or dating and no one is supposed to know?"

"Yeah, is there a no-dating policy at Alaska's Treasures tours?" Lisa asked, her face alight with curiosity.

"No on all counts."

Shelly looked thoughtful. "I've got it! You *used* to date, didn't you?"

What was the use of hiding it? "Yes, we used to date. But it was a long time ago." There was nothing else for her to do but admit it, even though it wasn't any of their business. Shelly and Lisa had "starry-eyed romance" beaming in their eyes as they gaped at her. She glanced in Nate's direction, and wouldn't you know, he looked up at about that time and their gazes locked.

The air seemed to suddenly electrify in that moment.

She yanked her gaze away and found herself staring at two sets of knowing eyes.

"Just as I thought. Unresolved love," Shelly said sighing.

"You can say that again," Lisa added. "How long has this been going on?"

Bethany would have laughed if she wasn't so bewildered. "I'd really rather not discuss this. It happened a long time ago. I just moved back into town a few days ago—"

"Oh," Lisa exclaimed. "That is so exciting. You've been gone, but now you're back and it looks like things could get wildly interesting."

Shelly smiled at the younger woman's enthusiasm. "I have a feeling Bethany and Nate may not resolve everything so easily. Am I right?"

"You are absolutely right. For one, he doesn't love me, so there is nothing to resolve." Why had she added that bit of info? If they only knew the half of it— which they wouldn't.

Lisa rested her chin on her knuckles and dipped her brows. "If that man doesn't love you, then he must be a very intense man."

"He is." Bethany didn't need this type of speculation. Of course, Lisa was in love and flying high on cloud nine, so of course she would imagine love blooming everywhere.

"So why did you move back?" Shelly asked.

"I'm a wedding planner."

"Oh!" Lisa exclaimed. "How fun. I had a blast planning my wedding. We didn't do it up real fancy, just a country wedding at my little church in Texas, but I loved it."

"I love country weddings. I've planned huge weddings and small weddings." Thankfully, the talk of weddings distracted them from focusing on her and Nate. For the next hour, they chattered about weddings like old friends. She told them about her new space and how women were already making appointments. She almost said even women without grooms were planning weddings, but decided not to mention that. She hoped Delilah found a groom, and she hoped Joleen was making progress with Harry. She watched Nate help Ely get a fish off his line.

"You're looking at him again," Lisa said.

"What?" Bethany asked.

"Nate. You've been watching him almost the entire time we've been talking. It looks like love to me," she said, teasing.

Bethany gave a dismissive laugh. "You're the one in love. Not me."

"Maybe," Shelly said, jumping back on the bandwagon. "But you're kidding yourself if you think there's nothing there."

"It's time to hit the last leg of the trail," Nate called, as the men gathered up their poles.

Bethany jumped from the rock and grabbed her backpack, as though it was time to abandon a sinking ship. "We will have to push hard to make it to the cabin before dark."

"Do you think the temperature is going to hold out?" Shelly asked, changing subjects.

"This forty-five-degree weather is fine, but if it drops lower I'm going to worry about having brought Cody out here."

"The outlook has been good so far. We don't even have rain on the forecast, and that's unusual for this late in the season. And even though the temperature will drop tonight, we'll be inside." Cody was hardly noticing the weather. "Relax, look at that boy. The brisk weather isn't hurting him."

Cody was jumping beside his dad as they headed toward the horses. He would sleep well tonight. So would they all, she was pretty sure…at least she hoped *she* could. The last thing she wanted to do was have a sleepless night, thinking of Nate.

Was it really so clearly visible in her expression how she'd felt about him all those years ago?

She was going to have to work on that. The last thing she wanted was Nate thinking she was still pinning away over the likes of *him*.

* * *

They made it to the cabins just before nightfall.

Bethany helped Ely set up the women's cabin, while Lisa sat on a log and watched. Her hip had stiffened up a bit, but she assured Bethany that she was fine. The girl wasn't a complainer. That was apparent. She was really a great sport.

Nate kept his distance—and it was a good thing, because she still hadn't gotten over what had happened that afternoon, and she'd rather not try to make conversation with him.

He spent the first thirty minutes taking care of the horses, then he began to start a campfire. Bethany headed out to get wood. That would keep her busy for at least a few minutes.

"Where ya goin'?" Cody asked. He was watching his parents put their gear in the cabins.

"To get firewood."

"Can I help?"

"Sure you can if it's okay with your parents," Bethany said.

"That's great. We'll help, too," Robert said. "Just as soon as we get through here."

"Yesss," Cody shouted, pumping his small fist in the air as he'd probably seen someone do.

Bethany chuckled at his enthusiasm. "With that kind of energy, we should have a bonfire within minutes."

They headed off into the woods. Cody walked beside her, picking up sticks as he saw them. "You think the bears will come to camp?"

Bethany bent to grab a tree limb. "We shouldn't have any trouble with the bears."

She could see the bears were quickly becoming an obsession. "You don't need to be afraid."

"I'm not afraid. My daddy wouldn't let one get to me. You think they might come get the horses, though?" He wasn't worried about himself, but he was worried about the horses.

"They'll be fine. Nate is watching out for them. Besides, those horses would make enough noise to wake us all up if any wild animal decided to bother them."

"Yeah, they would snort and whinny like Lisa's horse did."

Bethany smiled reassuringly at him. "That's exactly what they would do. I promise."

He looked as if he was trying to convince himself of this. "I'm gonna go tell my dad you said that." Turning, he headed toward where Robert and Shelly had started picking up tree limbs a few feet through the woods. Bethany watched him make his way to them, and then she went back to picking up more wood.

She was thinking about Nate and how she couldn't let herself weaken around him. Her arms full, she headed back. She couldn't see Robert, Shelly and Cody, but she knew they were close enough to camp not to get lost.

She'd just stepped into the camp area when she heard the horses getting excited about something on the far end of camp.

From where she was standing, she couldn't see them. She saw Nate come out of his cabin, then glance her way and headed off without a word. She dropped her wood and followed him. They spotted Cody at the same time. The kid was standing in the middle of the seven horses, trying to hang onto the lead rope of one of the horses he'd obviously just untied.

"What are you doing?" Nate roared, rushing forward to grab the rope from his small fingers.

"I was gonna move the horses closer to the cabins," Cody said, looking worried. "They want to be closer to us."

Nate tied the reins back to the rope he'd stretched between two trees and gently lifted Cody to the other side of the rope so he wouldn't be harmed if the horses got spooked. "They're fine right here Cody."

"But are you sure?"

Bethany wasn't certain how to take

Cody's behavior. She'd thought he was fine with her explanation earlier, and then this. Not to mention the fact that he was supposed to have been with his parents. It didn't take but one glance from Nate to tell her he was holding her responsible for this. "Cody, the horses will be fine. But you were supposed to be with your parents."

"I told them I was picking up wood with you, but then I got to thinking about the horses and came to take care of them instead."

"Well, it's nice that you're so concerned about the horses, but you could have been hurt, standing in the middle of all of them. Will you promise me you will be careful and not come near the horses, or wander around in the woods, without one of us with you? This is really serious, Cody. You could be harmed. Promise me you won't do this again."

He looked at his feet, kicking a golden leaf with his boot. "I promise."

"Good. Now let's go find your parents

and tell them what just happened." She stood up and took his hand.

"Come back here when you're done, Bethany," Nate said, gravely.

"You got it," she said.

She took Cody to Shelly and Robert and explained quickly, and then headed back to Nate. He was mad at her, no doubt about Cody, and she deserved it. Her heart was still racing at the sight of the little boy in the middle of the horses. Careless is what she'd been.

"I'm sorry," she said, the instant she got back to Nate.

He stalked to the opposite side of the horses, out of range of the camp. "How many times do I have to tell you that that boy needs constant supervision? He is your primary responsibility out here despite his parents being here. Can't you tell that he doesn't take direction more than half the time?"

"Yes, I know that." She didn't tell him that he was supposed to have been with his parents. That served no purpose. She had been in the wrong because she should have double-checked, made certain that he was with them before she left them in the woods.

"If you know that then why is he constantly where he isn't supposed to be? You know how important this is."

"Because," she said defensively.

"Because what?" He stepped close.

She looked up at him and her frustration took over. "Because I'm distracted by your behavior. I'm not doing my job because I can't figure out what is going on with you. I can't figure you out, period."

The angry glitter in Nate's blue eyes stalled as he stared at her. "I'm not that hard to figure out. I want that child safe. He's the reason you're on this trip. I'll be searching for signs the next couple of days with this treasure map from Amy. I can't be worrying that you aren't holding up your end of the deal."

That hit her wrong. So wrong. "You are asking me if I'm going to be trustworthy enough to hold up my end of the deal?" Of all the things he could have said, that one pushed her buttons like nothing else could. He nodded, and it was like a hammer slamming the nail home. "Give me a break," she snapped, stepping into his space. "It seems to me that if anyone can't hold up the end of a deal it's you. If I commit to something—and I have where this tour is concerned—then I'm going to honor my end of the deal. You, on the other hand, toss out promises, expectations that you have no intention of upholding, so don't give me this holier-than-thou spiel. This was an honest—if you know what that means— *mistake* where Cody is concerned, but you can be sure it won't happen again."

Spinning away, her face hot, she headed back to camp on weak legs. His hand on her arm halted her.

"Bethany—"

She needed to cool down and she knew it. His hand was strong on her arm, and instantly she was embarrassed by her behavior earlier, when she'd wanted him to kiss her. Brother!

"What?" she asked again, her voice coming out in a low whisper, as she fought tangling emotions. There had been a time when she'd thought God was smiling on her with the blessing of Nate's love—*stop,* she ordered herself.

"Bethany," his deep voice was gritty as he said her name.

She shook her head, backed away from him and willed herself to not humiliate herself again. "This is business, Nate. Let's keep it that way. I'll put on a show for them." She jerked her head toward camp. "But we don't need to pretend."

She wasn't sure how to read the way his eyes narrowed and his jaw tightened. Was he thinking she was overreacting? Did he think she was crazy? It didn't matter. This was business and nothing more. This was supposed to be her getting *over* Nate, not her throwing herself under the bus!

Chapter Eight

"I'm so sorry," Shelly said, the minute Bethany reached them. "This is exactly what I was worried about when I agreed to come on this trip. Cody gets distracted easily. I feel like I'm not doing a very good job, sometimes."

Bethany gave her a hug and tried to let go of the tension shrouding her. For Amy's tour company, she had to do right by her clients. Dragging them into this thing between her and Nate wouldn't be right. Totally unprofessional. And she'd learned never to be that in her business.

Planting on a smile, she tried to ease Shelly's concerns. "We will just have to be more aware, and if he's with me, then I won't take my eyes off of him until I see that he is with you. And you do the same. That way, we will both know he's where he is supposed to be," she said, as Nate walked up looking like a volcano about to explode. "And that will make our grumpy leader extremely happy, since your safety is his direct responsibility," she added brightly, strictly for the camper's benefit. But also because, despite her personal problem with Nate, this part was true.

Robert had been speaking quietly with Cody, and now they approached. Cody looked up at Nate with serious eyes. "I'm sorry for wandering off and going to the horses by myself."

Nate shifted his weight from one boot to the other. If he'd had on his cowboy boots instead of his hiking boots he'd have been classic cowboy, as he shifted his shoulders and touched the rim of his hat—a cowboy's way of giving himself a second to gather his thoughts. "You could have been harmed by the horses, son." He knelt beside the wood and prepared to light it. "That's all I'm worried about."

"I'm worried about the horses," Cody repeated, without skipping a beat.

Bethany sank onto a log and patted the seat beside her. "Let me tell you something about Nate. He is a cowboy and a wilderness guide, but he is also an animal rescue worker. Did you know that?"

Everyone moved to sit around the fire as it sparked to life. Cody's eyes widened. "You mean, you save animals?" he asked, as Nate pushed limbs around to catch the flame.

"Yes, I do."

Bethany knew she was on the right track for Cody's benefit. "So you see, Nate not only knows how to protect you, but he knows how to protect animals, too. He's not going to let anything happen to the horses."

Cody looked relieved. "What kinds of animals have you rescued?"

"All kinds of them. Bethany helped me rescue a baby moose one time."

"How?"

Nate grinned, taking this "let's get along for *their* sake" over the top. "She fell in the water trying to help pull it into the boat."

Nate chuckled, and despite everything, Bethany couldn't help smiling.

That had been quite a day. Nate had managed to fish her and the worn-out moose into the boat, then drive them to safety. The memory of how worried he'd been for her washed over her, just as Nate sat down on the log beside her—great, just what she did not need!

A walk down a memory lane of the good times they'd had was not what she intended when she'd brought up the subject of animal rescue.

Nate realized instantly that Bethany had found the way to ease Cody's mind. He felt bad about what he'd said and was disturbed by what she said. He gave her a tight smile, feeling bad and needing to apologize to her, but now wasn't the place. They were both experiencing the strain of this trip.

"I couldn't have saved that moose without her that day," he said, feeling as though he needed to fix what was going on between them, while not sure how to do it. They didn't used to fight, but it seemed the only thing they could do now.

He'd been blowing up or messing up with her at every turn, and it had to stop. Sitting here with the group, they could at least put on a pretense that all was okay between them.

"I bet it was funny to see Bethany and the moose in the water together," Cody said.

Nate remembered how worried he'd been. "It was a very dangerous situation Cody." Then, not wanting to totally scare the kid about the dangers of being outdoors, he added, "But yeah, it was something to see."

Bethany smiled at him and gave him a wink—really stretching the show. She obviously was worried that he'd been about to terrify the boy all over again by talking about how dire the situation had been.

Looking at her, he was glad he'd at least

done something right. It was a small thing, that wink, but his spirits lifted because of it. She'd made it clear earlier just how little she thought of him. In his mind, he'd done the right thing by setting her free from loving him…but knowing that she still harbored such bitter anger at him didn't fit right.

It didn't fit right at all.

"That's a big bird!" Cody exclaimed, the next morning, as Bethany pointed out a bald eagle soaring above them not long after they'd ridden out of camp. "Look at it, Mr. Nate."

He'd insisted on riding up front with Nate, and that had meant Bethany rode up front, too. Ever since she'd told Cody about him being an animal rescue responder, the little boy had looked at him like he was his favorite hero or something. It made Nate uncomfortable. But Bethany had been smart last night when she'd brought the subject up. It had eased the boy's worries over the horses, and it had also given them something to focus on other than the uncomfortable situation they were in.

They were managing better to carry the pretense of normalcy over this morning. The conversation around the fire had lessened the tension between them—to some degree. But he'd lain awake late into the night, thinking about the anger she'd shown when they were standing by the horses. He pushed the thoughts aside, though, and concentrated on what Cody was saying.

"It's pretty big," Nate said, pulling his horse to a halt, as he let the group watch the majestic eagle soar on the breeze. Its wingspan looked to be nearly ten feet across. There was nothing more beautiful than to watch an eagle gliding across the sky, especially being able to see its reflection on the emerald waters of the lake below them.

"His nest is probably in the trees, here on this lake," Bethany explained to Cody and the rest of the group. "From this point on, we will most likely see several eagles."

"Some might not look like bald eagles, since they don't get their white head until they are about four years old," Nate reminded them.

"So you might see some of this one's kids flying around out here," Bethany added, as Nate began leading the group forward again.

They all rode along, talking among themselves. Nate was very aware of Bethany behind him.

"I'm adopted," Cody said suddenly. "My mom and dad said I was special and that's why they wanted me. You got any special kids, Mr. Nate?"

Being waylaid by a seven-year-old boy was the last thing he'd expected. "Um, no," Nate managed. "I don't have any kids. I'm not married," he added.

"Why not? You're old like my dad. You're s'posed to have a wife, ain't ya?"

A startled sound came from Bethany and he caught her eye then looked away feeling trapped. The last thing he wanted to do was talk about not having kids in front of her. Or his lack of a wife.

"Not everyone gets married, Cody," Bethany offered.

Nate glanced at her again, relieved that she was helping avoid this subject. "Not everyone has kids."

"Why not?"

The kid was a persistent little tyke! "Oh, lots of reasons," Nate said, *praying* for a bear to step out and distract Cody.

Bethany shot Cody a dazzling smile. "You're special, all right, and your parents are very blessed to have you. One day, I'd love to have a little boy *just* like you. Do you think there's another little fella out there like you?"

Cody nodded, sitting up in his saddle excitedly. "There's plenty of 'em. I can remember them for you if you want me to."

On that one, Nate decided it was time to head out again. The number of children who needed good homes were mind-blowing. But Bethany could have her own children, and there was no way he was getting in the way of that happening…not that he felt she would ever let him back into her life. Her words last night had proved that she despised him and was only tolerating him until they got back to Treasure Creek.

But what had he expected?

Nate planned to be at the cliff by daybreak. He'd just finished getting the horses into the small corral beside the lean-to barn and was checking his climbing gear for the next morning when he planned to rappel down to the crevice. The soft sound of footsteps on grass signaled someone approaching, and he glanced over his shoulder just as Bethany stepped into the barn. She looked from him to the ropes and rappelling devices, and to his surprise, her eyes widened in alarm.

"Nate, no! I knew this was the same cabin near your grandfather's cliff, but I didn't realize—surely you aren't thinking about looking in there again?"

"I told you I was looking for signs of the treasure."

"But I just thought you were looking

around here for a cave entrance or something like that."

He laid the metal device down that would ensure his safety during the climb. "I am. But I'm thinking my grandfather figured that crevice was a cave entrance that connects topside around here. I'm on my way now to scout about and check out the cliff before I make my pass in the morning. I know you can handle getting everything set up for the night." He made certain he said she *could* and didn't make the mistake of questioning whether she could or not. Still, she didn't look happy.

"This is a bad idea. Are you sure you want to do this? You know the odds of that treasure being in that cave are remote. I had no idea you were planning on rappelling. Has Amy sanctioned this? It's too dangerous, especially alone."

It hit him that she was worried about him. "There is enough of a chance that I can't ignore it, if it could help the community. It's time I looked once more."

"But what if something happens? You

know as well as I do that it will take time to get a rescue crew in here."

"I'll be fine. Nothing is going to happen."

She crossed her arms and looked less than convinced. "Nate, I was there when you slipped before. Remember?"

Bethany had been a basket case when he'd slipped on the climb when he was eighteen. After it was over and he'd gotten his gear off, she'd been so mad at him that she almost broke up with him. She'd cried uncontrollably. He'd known he loved her that day. Known what it felt like to be cherished by a woman. "I remember," hc said, holding her gaze, wishing he could hug her close and whisper that everything was fine. "I'll be back, I promise," he mumbled past the frog that had lodged in his throat, as he strode out of the small barn and away from her. He headed to the edge of the pine trees, to the path that would lead him to the ravine.

Chapter Nine

"Here comes Nate!" Cody yelled, just before all daylight disappeared. He'd been asking about him all evening and watching the trail for his return. Now he tore across the yard, his little red coat a flash in the dusk. "Nate, whatcha been doing?"

Nate patted his shoulder as they fell into step. "Just looking at the trail. What have *you* been doing?"

"Helping Bethany get the fire going and stuff. I'm getting real good at it. You should have seen me."

"I'm proud of you. Your mom and dad are going to make a real mountain man out of you."

"Oh, yeah, I told them I want to grow up and do what you do. Rescue animals and climb mountains."

Despite her worries, Bethany smiled. It was obvious Cody adored him. Nate needed his own children.

"I think that's great. I know I've always enjoyed what I do." He looked kindly at Cody as he took a seat around the campfire with the rest of the group. Cody sat down on the log beside him.

Bethany was anxious to talk to Nate, but she didn't like how upset this was making her. Nate had always been such a dedicated hardworker. He'd loved his grandfather, and his death had haunted him. She'd known this when they were dating and had tried to get him to talk about it, but he wouldn't.

Nate McMann had been raised by men who felt that a man wasn't supposed to be vulnerable, and was supposed to be strong and honorable at all times.

It had been the last part that always got her—*how had breaking my heart been honorable?* The only thing she could come up with was that he'd realized telling her the truth was more honorable than living a lie. She guessed, as hard as it was, that he'd been right. She wouldn't have wanted to find out later that she'd been living a lie.

Most likely, Nate had honored his dad and granddad by breaking off their relationship. So what was she doing sitting here, worrying about him rappelling down the side of the cliff where his grandfather died. Nate didn't need her concern, and he certainly didn't need her trying to be a mother hen to him. She'd made it for five days, and if she could get through tomorrow she'd be back in Treasure Creek by nightfall—and this would be over. Treasure Creek might not be large, but it was huge compared to the confines of a group hike in the wilderness.

"We've had a great time," Robert said. "This experience has been our first vacation as a family, and," he slipped his arm around Shelly and they smiled at each other, "we've had so much fun, we may make it an annual tradition."

"That goes for us, too," Lisa said,

clutching Ely's hand. "Even with me falling off my horse." She looked pink in the firelight. "Seeing that bear is what I'll remember the most."

"Hey, what about me?" Ely teased, looking stricken.

"I meant, after *you,* the bear is what I'll remember the most."

"Ely, you know that's what she meant," Bethany teased.

They were a cute couple, a bit annoying with their public affection, but still adorable. Bethany would love to see them in a few years. She had a feeling they would be just as crazy about each other as they were now.

Everyone had a good time teasing the young couple over the next few minutes. They all talked about the different things they'd seen during the trip and how quickly it seemed to have come to an end. Nate reminded them that they still had another day to finish out before the van picked them up and carried them back to Treasure Creek.

Bethany realized that, rather than be excited to be free of Nate as she'd thought, the idea saddened her. It hit her as she stared across the campfire at him, that this might be the only chance she'd have to try and get answers to the questions that had plagued her all these years…but did she really want to push for clarity? Would he think she was still hurting after all these years? Even if it was true, did she want him to know that? The very thought had her sitting out on the porch later after everyone else had turned in for the night.

It was a cold, clear night. Tugging her coat close, she tucked the woven blanket around her legs and watched the northern sky. It was the perfect night for the northern lights to put on a show. She'd seen the aurora borealis many times growing up, but the night had to be just right for the beautiful lights to show up here, this far away from Anchorage.

The door creaked, and Nate walked out of the cabin. He didn't look her way, but closed the door after him and walked to the edge of the small porch. Just like that, the air seemed charged with electricity, and to Bethany's surprise she spied a glimmer of light radiating in the northern sky.

"We're about to see a light show," Nate said, staring at the distant threads of glowing green streaks eerily crossing the sky.

It was as if God had just taken a luminescent can of paint and tossed it across the Heavens in a swirling pattern. Bethany gasped at the beauty.

"I'm always amazed at how beautiful it is," she said quietly.

He nodded, still not looking at her. "'God showing off' is what my grandfather used to call it."

Feeling a chill, Bethany pulled her blanket closer. It was easy to feel distant from God, but watching the magnificent display of beauty made it far too hard to maintain that distant feeling. It was as if He were standing beside them saying "Watch this, I'm doing it just for the two of you."

She couldn't say that though, it would give away the feelings slugging away inside of her. How would she ever feel close to God again when she couldn't get past the resentment she felt? When she didn't say anything, Nate turned toward her. He was five feet from her, but the night was so alive with light that she could see him well.

"I know we are skirting around issues that deal with what I did to you ten years ago."

Bethany clasped her hands together tightly. This was unexpected. "It's to be expected," she said.

He gave a short laugh, more of a grunt than anything. "Yeah, you're right." He cleared his throat, shifted from boot to boot and looked uncomfortable. "Hurting you was the last thing I ever wanted to do."

Her heart felt as if it were in a vise grip. "I guess it couldn't be helped." Her knees were weak even sitting down. "The truth was the best thing, even if it did hurt." It was true, and they both knew it. The stricken look that the words brought to his expression confused her. He looked as if she'd just slapped him or something.

"Yeah, right," he grunted, turning back to watch the light show. "I guess we should get everyone, so they can see this."

Bethany couldn't face the group right now. "Why did your grandfather believe the treasure was hidden around here?" she asked, struggling. Changing the subject and using something she was really interested in seemed logical. She hated to deprive the group of seeing the northern lights, but she couldn't do anything else. Nate stepped off the porch and sat on the edge, obviously deciding the same thing.

"My grandfather grew up hearing stories from his dad about Amy's great, great grandfather. I thought I told you all of this."

"You did," she said, stilling the drumming of her heart. Relaxing a bit. "But it's been years since I thought about it, and I want a refresher. If I'm here, I need to understand it all."

"My grandfather heard the treasure map story from his dad. He talked of a cabin with an underground cave entrance near it.

The cave's other entrance was a crevice on the side of a cliff. Best we can figure is that grandfather found this place and believed it was the cave. When he couldn't find the entrance near the cabin he decided to lower himself down to the crevice."

"And your dad found this out only after reading it in your grandfather Chester's journal after his death, right?"

Nate nodded. "Chester had spent a lot time searching for the place, and Dad never knew it. Dad never believed there was an actual treasure. But…" Nate's words drifted off as he met her gaze and he gave an almost imperceptible shrug. "After being raised believing that a man's honor is everything, it bothers me to know dad doesn't put much merit in granddad's journal. It bothered me in high school and it bothers me now. Dad always believed that the real treasure here in these parts isn't the treasure that enticed people over the Chilkoot Trail, but the land itself. The beauty of the place—and being privileged to live here."

Bethany knew Nate believed that, too.

He also believed a man's honor was everything…again, that was what always bugged her the most. Nate was a man of honor, and even after he'd tore her heart out she'd not doubted it. But why had he strung her along?

Standing, restless and wobbly kneed, she walked to the far edge of the porch. The haunting sounds of night animals drifted on the cold breeze, echoing the past that still haunted her.

"Nate…"

She faced him across the ten feet between them. It was time to be bold and get to the heart of this. It was the only way to put it to rest. The only way for her to move forward. That was why she'd come back. Not in some pathetic hope that he would have come to his senses and realized that he really did love her after all. She came back to find out answers, before letting all hope of him go in her heart of hearts.

"Nate," she started over, having gathered her thoughts, "I've been distant from God ever since you broke up with me. I guess I blamed Him for your lack of love for me, and I lost the will to connect with Him. No, don't say anything," she said, when Nate opened his mouth to speak. "I need to say this. I came on this trip to have closure about what happened between us. Yes, I haven't had it all these years. I didn't take your rejection well, and I'll admit that it's been hard."

His jaw jerked and he looked away. "I'm sorry."

Bethany could distinctly hear the sincerity there. "I know, looking back, that I may have been part of the problem. I mean, we were young, and I did have conflicting dreams. You probably felt overwhelmed by my plans to pursue a career that meant leaving Treasure Creek behind. And then for me to talk almost in the same breath about marrying you and having children—I guess I just expected us to be able to do it all. I guess I just believed you could give up all of this, and that life with me would be enough."

He didn't say anything, just kept staring

out at the northern lights. "I'm trying to say I'm sorry for my childish thoughtlessness." She laughed harshly at a truth she'd never liked.

Nate stood up abruptly. "Don't ever apologize for that. You had dreams. I loved your drive, your energy—" his earnest words halted, as he yanked his hat off and crammed his hand through his blonde hair.

He looked so youthful in that moment— the young man she'd loved so much. Hardworking and earnest, he'd wanted to be just like his dad and grandfather. She knew when she'd fallen in love with him that their life goals weren't compatible, but she'd been unable to stop herself.

He was all about the ranch—breaking horses, working cattle and carrying on the family legacy; she on the other hand wanted to see the world by doing weddings all over the globe. But that took sacrifice and hard work building a name in a large city such as San Francisco.

In her naive mind she'd assumed love would work everything out.

A thought struck her. It was a faint glow of almost untouchable hope…surely not—it had been Nate that worked her future dreams out when he'd changed his mind about loving her. When he'd walked away, there remained only one unhindered path for her to take. He wouldn't have told her he didn't love her so that she would go to San Francisco…*would he?*

Staring at him now, her stomach churned and she felt sick. He'd changed his mind so quickly. And he was still single—did that mean anything?

Blood rushed to her head and pounded in her temples. She closed her eyes against the pain. Nate believed in being an honorable man. He wouldn't have lied to her. He wouldn't have hurt her like that, even if he thought he was doing the right thing.

Would he? She stared at him in disbelief.

"I, um, better turn in," he said, looking as shaken as she felt as he strode to the door. "I

have an early morning. You coming? I—"
He cleared his throat, not meeting her eyes.
"I don't really like leaving you out here by
yourself this late."

Bethany didn't move. Couldn't move. "I'll
be in shortly," she managed to say. "Don't
worry about me."

His brows crinkled and he inhaled
sharply, meeting her eyes with his pain-
filled ones. She thought he was about to
say more, when he nodded, pushed the door
open and left her alone on the porch.

Alone with the first viable reason of merit
for his devastating actions so long ago….
She stared at the closed door, dazed by
this new bit of the puzzle. It confused her
more.

There was no way she was getting any
sleep tonight. And the only reason she
hadn't said something to him was out of
self-preservation. She had to know how she
felt about this before she asked him if this
revelation had any truth to it. If he shocked

her and told her it did, what exactly did that mean to her?

What did she want it to mean?

Chapter Ten

Had he taken the coward's way out? Nate asked himself the question over and over the next morning. He'd reached the top of the cliff, working his way from a lower trail from the cabin upward, toward the top of the cliff. He studied the side of the mountain as he went, seeing the dark crevice that he would be lowering himself down to.

His thoughts churned with things from the night before that had left him questioning himself. He'd always believed, as his dad did that hard work and a man's honor were the most important things in life. If a man didn't have honor, then he wasn't much of a man. Nate couldn't stop thinking about

Bethany—had he been wrong to let her go without telling her why? Should he have told her the truth? Was telling her he didn't love her the cowards way out? The thought was a punch in the gut.

He told himself all these years that the lie had been the only way. That God understood that a man had to do what a man had to do. But his conscience pricked.

He reached the top of the cliff and stood on the edge of the rock and looked down. It was basically a straight drop, with rough areas on the face. His grandfather had made this drop, determined to see if his hunch was right about the treasure's hiding place. He made the drop with makeshift equipment and lack of experience, and he'd died because of it.

Nate pulled his rappelling gear from his backpack. He chose a solid tree with deep roots, and set to work anchoring his rope around it securely. Bethany's concerned face hovered in his mind as he worked. She'd looked as if she still cared. The thought made his internal conflicts even that much harder to counter.

She'd come here for closure. Not looking to reopen their past. Not hoping to take up where they'd left off. But for closure. She hadn't been able to move forward any more than he had. Closure was best for both of them.

If she got married, it would help bring closure to him.

If she loved someone else he wouldn't feel this temptation to tell her the truth. His hands shaking, he pulled on his harness and tightened the straps. He couldn't tell her.

It would serve no purpose. None at all.

"Are you sure this is the way he went?"

Bethany nodded at Ely. She hadn't been able to stand the thought of Nate out there, climbing around the mountain with no one else around. She'd been about to head out after him when both Ely and Robert had come outside and asked her where Nate had gone.

Bethany had never been so happy to see

two people in all her life. Worried, she'd quickly told them what Nate was doing and asked if they would hike to the rock face with her. Both agreed, and after Robert had alerted Shelly where they were going, they'd headed out after Nate.

He was about thirty minutes ahead of them, but she knew he'd have to get his gear together before he made his way over the edge of the cliff. She hoped they would get there before he did it. Just the thought of him hanging on the side of that cliff by a rope made her sick.

She'd never been one to think any kind of rock climbing was good. She didn't have the disposition for it. Especially thinking about someone she loved taking the chance of plunging to his death—and yes, despite all the reasons why she shouldn't, she knew that she still loved Nate McMann.

She'd lain awake most of the night after she went to bed, and thought long and hard about how she felt about him. And also about her startling hunch that he might have broken her heart so that she wouldn't have to choose between him or her career. Had he done that?

The very idea infuriated her. And the more she thought about it the more it fit. He'd known in his heart that he wouldn't be going to San Francisco, or any other large city where she would need to go to make it big in the wedding industry. Knowing him like she did, she also knew, looking back, that there would have been no way that he would have asked her to give up her dream. No way at all. How had she not realized this?

Had she been too tied up in her pain to realize it at first—and then too tied up in her anger at him after that to see past the resentment she felt? It made sense.

It was her only explanation. And she couldn't figure out how to react to it—even if she was wrong. The only thing she knew was that Nate was alone on the mountain, and she couldn't stand the thought.

Did she love him still?

Yes.

But that would forever remain her secret.

It was one thing to acknowledge it, but an entirely different thing to let him know. Following him now was simply out of concern for him. It would tell him nothing more.

Robert and Ely were concerned for him, too. That was why they'd gotten up. When they'd heard him get dressed, then pick up his backpack full of rappelling gear—which they'd seen him going over the night before—they'd been curious about what he was doing. She felt strength from their support and concern for him.

"This is the way," she said, knowing the path as though it had been only yesterday that she'd come this way, and not over ten years ago. This spot had torn Nate up as a teenager. "This was one of the last trails I hiked with Nate before I left Treasure Creek. A few more feet and you'll be able to see the rock face. Hopefully, he's not to the top yet and we can get there before he secures his rope and drops over the edge."

As she spoke, they emerged through the dense woods. Morning sunlight sparkled like gold dust on the morning haze. Ahead of them, the rock face rose from the low fog, hovering over the valley that sloped off from where they were standing. From here, the hike was easy, going down into the valley below them toward the slow-moving river.

But upward, to the top of the majestic rock face, was a steep, but very accessible climb to those who were moderately in shape.

Bethany's gaze went immediately to movement at the top of the cliff just as Nate turned and began walking backwards down the side of the mountain. His rappelling rope swung below him as he worked his way down it, letting it slide through the metal clamp on the harness he wore around his hips.

Her heart lunged into her throat and she couldn't move. But she could pray. Quickly but fervently, she asked God to keep him safe.

"There he goes," Ely said, excitement in his voice. "He'll be okay, Bethany. Nate knows what he's doing."

Robert patted her shoulder. "He doesn't strike me as a man who would do something foolish. From here, it looks like he knows what he's doing."

"He does. I didn't mean to make you think otherwise. It's just that things happen, and he shouldn't be doing this alone." Both men gave her curious looks. She shut up, knowing full well what they were thinking, and put her attention on the small figure of Nate a hundred and eighty feet above the floor of the valley. Her insides quivered with apprehension. Her mouth had gone dry the minute she spotted him. She stared at the narrow crevice fifty feet below him. "Nate's grandfather believed that crack in the side of the rock was a cave."

Robert watched Nate. "Does this have anything to do with the rumor I heard in town before we left, about a treasure that is supposed to be hidden somewhere out here? I heard it had something to do with the owner of the tour company."

"Yeah," Ely said, staring at her with eyes that were no longer worried, but filled with the excitement. "Like it belonged to her grandfather or something, back in the gold rush days, and he hid it for some strange reason. Personally, I don't believe it. I told Lisa a man wouldn't bury a treasure."

"Unless it was the safest thing to do." Robert gave a short laugh. "You have to remember, back then there were cutthroats roaming around, ready to pounce on anyone they thought might have a little gold. Maybe he hid it and planned to come back for it later."

"Maybe he planned that. But for whatever reason, Nate's grandfather died trying to find it up there." Bethany couldn't take her eyes off of Nate as he reached the opening and slipped inside. Her head was hurting from the strain of worry. She could see light illuminate the darkness and knew he had his flashlight out. She should have relaxed while he wasn't dangling off the rock, but she couldn't. Within minutes, he was back out giving Bethany a case of hives as he shoved away from the rock face in a wide arch before his feet connected to the wall like a cat pouncing.

Before, when he'd almost plunged to his death like his grandfather, Nate hadn't had any experience, and he'd made a careless mistake. Today he looked perfect. He was beautiful coming down the wall. Bethany started into the valley and Robert and Ely followed her. She wanted to be there when he touched ground.

"I think I might want to learn how to do that one day," Ely said, hurrying behind her.

"Not me," Robert said. "I love my family too much to take a chance like that."

"I'm sure Shelly and Cody are glad about that." She didn't even acknowledge Ely's declaration, and had no doubt whatsoever that if he even mentioned it to Lisa she'd curb the idea in an instant. There was something, though, about Nate that was untamable—if he wanted to throw himself off the side of a cliff, to dangle at the mercy of a little piece of metal and a rope, then he'd do it. Of course, he didn't have anyone at home keeping the home fires burning. So why was she all worked up? Why was she as hot as a grease fire when she pushed through the last thicket that was in her way and found him coiling up his rope?

"What are y'all doing out here?"

"We were worried about you being out here by yourself," Robert said, giving him a hardy clap on the back. "Accidents can happen, even to the best climbers."

"I'm fine," Nate said, his words clipped.

"Did you see anything up there?" Ely asked.

"Nothing." Nate slid a glance to Bethany. His jaw was tight and his gaze held deep disappointment.

"So it's not a cave after all?" she asked quietly. She hadn't wanted him to do this, but she hadn't wanted him to be wrong either. This was important to him.

"No. Nothing. There isn't anything there but a crack in the rock that ends in the one fairly shallow area. I didn't miss anything when I came here the first time."

Bethany heard the underlying truth of his words, a truth neither Ely nor Robert could hear given the fact that she hadn't told them everything. "I'm sorry," she said, placing her hand on his arm in an attempt at comfort. She knew he was thinking once more that his grandfather had died for nothing.

"Let's head back," he said. "We'll be late getting the horses to the pickup zone and meeting the van, if we don't get started soon."

Ely grinned, oblivious. "I'll lead the way."

Robert shook his head and looked back at Bethany and Nate, as Ely strode off, leaving them to follow. "You better watch your back Nate, this one just might try to take your job when we get back to civilization. Ely's turned into a regular mountain man."

Despite his glum mood, Nate chuckled at the idea. "I'll make sure to do that."

His chuckle did Bethany's heart good. She held back as Robert followed Ely. "Are you okay," she whispered. "I mean really?"

"I'm fine. Been better, but fine. Why did you bring them out here?"

"Like I said, they followed you outside and found me thinking about following you." She left it at that, not feeling that she had to explain why they'd come after him.

They'd crossed a steep, moss-covered incline on their way into the valley. She and Nate had just reached a point where they could see Ely up ahead of them as he began walking across the tricky path. Bethany was just about to call out and tell him to slow down, when his foot hit a slick spot in the moss. One moment Ely was standing in front of them, the next his feet flipped out from under him, and he was sliding and rolling down the slick, mossy slope. Yelling all the way down.

Helpless, Bethany, Nate and Robert could only watch him go. He rolled the last little bit, hit a slight hump and took air at the base, before flying into the bushes. Nate was moving instantly, half jogging, half sliding on the rubber soles of his boots.

Robert followed suit and Bethany did the same, only slower. If they all crashed and broke their legs getting to the bottom, there would be no one to go for help. She took the more cautious choice, just in case.

Nate had just reached the thicket when Ely came crawling out. His face was ashen. *"Body—"*

Scrambling to get on his feet, he was having trouble, and Nate took one arm, helping him as he pointed back behind him with the other. "Body," he said. "There's a body in the b-bushes!"

Chapter Eleven

Eli wasn't joking. Nate went into the thicket and confirmed his finding. Poor Ely went to the edge of the woods and threw up several times. Nate asked Robert to escort him back to the camp and to take charge of everything, while he and Bethany went to call in the body to Reed Truscott, the town sheriff.

"Do you think this could be Tucker?"

Nate rubbed his jaw and looked grim. "I hope not," he shook his head and stared momentarily at his boots. "But the body, though badly decomposed, looks like a man about the same size as Tucker. Come on, I need to hike back to the top of the cliff and get an emergency call out to Reed and Gage."

They were quiet as they made their way up the slippery slope. Bethany kept thinking about the man they'd both gone to school with. Tucker Lawson had been a year ahead of them in school, and he'd left town right after he graduated because he and his widowed dad didn't get along. "Did Tucker ever make up with his dad?" she asked, her heart was heavy with sadness about the whole situation.

Nate took her hand and pulled her along behind him, up a particularly steep section of the climb. "No. He never came back until the funeral. As far as I know, the rift was still there."

"That's horrible. Life is too short."

"Yeah, it is," Nate said, and his quiet answer seemed to echo as they emerged from the dense trees into the open area at the base of the rock face. Nate let go of her hand and she followed him along the path leading up to the top. It was only about eight o'clock, but it seemed like they'd been out here for ages. Nate took the trail at a fast clip and she stayed with him. She knew it would be an all-day affair for the rescue team to get here and get the body out, and they would need all the daylight available to them. She was quiet as she followed him, not wanting to slow him down.

"Jake Rodgers is going to take this hard," he said, after a few minutes. "He's been holding out hope that Tucker is still alive."

"And he may still be. This might not be him."

"You're right. And I don't mean to sound negative, but the reality is that more than likely it is."

She knew he was right, but there was still a chance.…

Even so, if it wasn't, then who was it? They'd reached the halfway mark and he stopped to pull out his phone, glanced at it and started forward again. It was amazing how many people came into the wilderness and didn't realize that they wouldn't have phone access at any given time. Bethany had actually begun to take being connected for granted until this tour, and though she hadn't given it much thought, she realized that she'd enjoyed time spent without the phone connection. Life here in Alaska was different than life in the lower forty-eight, there was no denying it. Despite the grim situation, she smiled, thinking about how easily she was adapting to the idea of spending the rest of her life here in Treasure Creek. She'd come home.

"So, are you all right?" Shelly asked Bethany, a few hours after they'd made it back to camp. Bethany had been sitting on a fallen tree trunk, off to the edge of camp, waiting for the rescue team to arrive, and Shelly had come to join her. "You've been awfully quiet since you got back. It's understandable. I mean, that *is* a dead body out there."

This was all true, but it wasn't the dead body that had her being quiet. "I'm fine. I mean, I'm praying for whoever this person is and for his family, too." It was true she was praying. "But…" Bethany paused and watched Cody playing catch with Robert on the far side of clearing. "Shelly, can I ask you a personal question?"

"Sure, fire away."

Bethany met her curious brown eyes and smiled hesitantly. "Okay, I want a child. I've wanted children all my life, and I'm getting older and I'm still not married. Today it hit me that I've come back to Treasure Creek and discovered that this is home. This is the place I want to raise a family, and I'm tired of waiting on the right man to come along to make my family a reality. I was sitting here, contemplating the idea of adopting a child on my own. What do you think about that?"

Shelly looked thoughtful as she let Bethany's words sink in. "I know you'd be a wonderful mother. Waiting is frustrating, to say the least. It was so hard for me. But, why give up on a husband so soon?"

"So *soon?* Shelly I'm *twenty-nine,* with no prospects in sight."

Shelly chuckled. "That's not old. And

believe me, you have prospects. A major one is on this hike with us."

"No, Nate is not a prospect."

She knew by the way Shelly's eyes widened that she heard the frustration in her voice.

"You sound so positive about that, when all of us can tell there is still something going on between the two of you."

Bethany couldn't take it any more. "I once loved Nate with all my heart. We planned to marry after high school, but he broke up with me right after graduation, telling me he didn't love me. This thing you see between us is tension. He broke my heart without any explanation, and so I moved away." She stopped, wondering if she sounded like a whiner. "I… I've been busy with my career, but I've also never been able to move on." There—she'd admitted it to someone.

"So now I get it." Shelly exclaimed softly. "There is truly unfinished business here, just as Lisa and I thought. Really, Bethany, you need to just relax and give this time. God will work it out for you."

Bethany hid her frustration at this. God hadn't worked it out yet. "I'm tired of waiting."

Shelly placed a hand on her wrist. "I've been there. Really I have. I was thirty-three and not married myself. I, too, had given up on finding a husband who would marry me, knowing I could never have children. And believe me when I tell you that I was more than a bit angry at God about the entire situation. Angry and resentful and getting bitter. And then, out of the blue, Robert walked into my life and we were married within the year.

"We've only been married four years. We've been foster parents for three of those years, seeing children come through our home who really needed a stable environment and love. We were blessed even before Cody came into our life last year. God's timing amazes me when I look back over it. I mean, think about it. If I'd married someone earlier, I wouldn't have met Robert— and he is my life.

"If I'd been able to have children of my

own, I might not have been open to foster care or adoption...and then I wouldn't have been there when Cody needed me. And he needed me and Robert so badly. He's a drug baby, which is part of his attention problem. And he was basically just thrown away by his parents. Just tossed out like he was nothing...he was three and living in an abandoned house by himself, starving when the police found him and put him in foster care.

"When he came to us last year, he'd been in six different foster homes. He was troubled and needed me. And I knew my life, and every bit of waiting I'd done, had been worth it so that I could be there to love Cody.

"Bethany, don't blame God. Instead, be patient and pray for Him to lead you in the decision you make. Adopting on your own might be what He has in mind for you. But maybe He has something else in store for you."

Cody turned and waved at Shelly. "Mom, come play," he called. Shelly hugged her tightly. "God has a plan for you and it's wonderful. I know it. So hang in there."

Bethany watched Shelly jog to Cody and swing him around in her arms before placing him on the ground and letting him toss her the ball.

What an amazing story. It made her feel ungrateful in many ways. Bowing her head, she prayed an earnest prayer that God would lead her to the future *He* had planned for her.

Police chief Reed Truscott and Gage Parker arrived just after lunch to take charge of the body. Because of the turn of events, the delay finding the body caused the tour to be late getting the horses back to the pickup stop and meeting the van. They'd had to ride harder than Nate liked, but they needed to beat the darkness.

Ely and Lisa had opted to catch a ride with the search-and-rescue helicopter. Ely had been pretty shaken up after discovering the body, and Nate could understand why. Robert and Shelly had decided to finish out the last leg of the tour and help them get the horses to the pickup spot, where a truck and trailer waited to carry them all back to civilization.

Nate was more than glad when the van pulled up in front of the tour company office.

"Thanks for a great time," Robert said, as he shook Nate's hand and prepared to climb into the SUV and drive his family to the airport. "Could you let us know who the body is? It wasn't exactly the end of the tour that we'd planned, but the rest of the tour was great."

Nate held out his hand and they shook. "You were a great help in this difficult situation. Extraction is never a pleasant thing to do. Thank you. Not everyone would have offered to help us transport the body."

"I'm just glad I could help. Thanks for spending time with Cody. He thinks you hung the moon."

"He's a good kid."

And he was. Nate watched Cody talking to Shelly and Bethany. His expression was animated as they discussed the different things they'd seen on the tour. The bear, to be exact.

"We should head out and let them finish up here," Robert said to Shelly.

She hugged Bethany. "You hang in there and don't give up on God."

"I will. And thank you for everything. I'll keep in touch."

Nate didn't know what they'd talked about, but he could tell by the look in Bethany's eyes that it had been important. Bethany had been unusually quiet on the trip back to town. He watched as she bent down and hugged Cody, and he didn't miss the tears that glistened in her eyes. It twisted his insides. She'd gotten attached to the little boy quickly. For someone he thought would have at least one child by now, he wondered how she felt about that.

As they finished loading up, Bethany stepped back to stand beside him, waving as the Taylors' taillights disappeared into the night.

"They were great," he said, feeling

awkward. The tour was over, so now they would have no reason to have to face each other. "Thanks for all your help. Amy was correct that you were the right person for the tour. You were great with Cody, and I'm sorry I was so hard on you. I couldn't have done this without you."

She blinked in the light from the street lamp, and startled him with a chuckle. "Thank you. I know that had to be hard for you to admit."

He nodded, not smiling, feeling too shredded inside. She had no idea how being near her was tearing him up. He needed to head to his truck and get out of town and as far away from her as possible.

With the Taylors gone they were alone. Nate needed to burn rubber getting out of the parking lot and away from Bethany. He needed to—

"Do you want to go get some supper at Lizbet's?"

That he didn't need to do!

She took a deep breath, glancing down the street to the bright lights of the diner.

It was getting late, and the place was more than likely getting ready to shut down within the hour. "I'm tired and grungy. I'm really ready to go back to my room."

"Me, too. But we have to eat." Why was he pushing this?

She shook her head and her shoulders slumped. "I don't think so. Not tonight."

"You sure?" Disappointment curled inside of him when she nodded. It dawned on him then that she didn't have a car. "Then I'll just give you a ride to the hotel."

"That I'll take. Thank you. I'm going to have to buy a car, now that I'll be getting settled. The one I had in San Francisco wouldn't have been practical here, so I sold it."

"I'll be glad to take you wherever you need to go." Nate grabbed both backpacks and tossed them into the bed of his truck, then opened the passenger door and waited while Bethany scooted into the seat. In the interior light, he could see the dark circles under her eyes that he hadn't noticed earlier. She hadn't been sleeping.

"Thank you," she said, as he closed the door.

He nodded, then jogged around to his side and slid behind the wheel. "Where to?"

"Treasure Creek Hotel. I'm staying there until my things arrive for my apartment."

Nate headed that way, wishing it was farther away than two blocks.

"I actually need to go by my shop and pick up my suitcase. I checked out of the hotel for the week that we were on the trail, and I just made new reservations to start up again tonight."

"That was a good idea." He made the right-hand turn and pulled the truck to a stop in front of her shop.

"It was actually the manager's idea. He had someone who desperately needed a room for a couple of nights and asked me if he could store my things and rent the room while I was gone. I decided that was a great idea, and I brought my cases over here so they would be out of their way."

The streetlight illuminated the white

exterior and big window. Nate checked out the length of the street, deserted this time of night. Treasure Creek was a safe little town generally speaking, but it never hurt to be cautious. He followed her to the door. "I'll get that bag for you."

She got the door opened then clicked the light switch. Bright light filled the space.

"This is a nice space." He tipped his hat back and studied the room.

"Thanks. I think it will work perfectly. And I'm moving into the apartment upstairs when my things arrive. Hopefully, that will be tomorrow. They promised me for certain it would be here by then. This is the one I want," she said, pointing at a medium-size suitcase sitting beside a larger one. He grabbed it while she picked up an overnight bag.

He wasn't ready to go, and wished he could draw out the conversation for as long as possible. But he couldn't. She was tired and already heading outside. It was apparent that she didn't want to spend any more time with him than necessary.

They were quiet as he drove the short distance to the hotel. "I'll carry your bags in if you want to go ahead and get checked in."

"Thanks." She was gone in a flash. His feet were dragging as he grabbed the two bags and followed her. He entered the old, historic hotel a few minutes later, and met her coming toward him with a tight expression of bewilderment.

"They got my reservation mixed up and have me down for tomorrow. No rooms available tonight. With all the fancy women in town, he's booked up. I have nowhere to stay!"

Nate smiled inside and knew he was in trouble feeling that way. It didn't stop him from opening his big mouth, "Sure you do. You can stay at my place."

Chapter Twelve

"I can't stay at your place," Bethany was quick to point out. "Thanks, but that just isn't acceptable."

"You can stay at the guest house is what I meant. There's no one there, and Sue keeps it ready for unexpected guests. And you wanted to see her anyway."

Bethany didn't look convinced. "Nate, this isn't a good idea."

"You need a place to stay. It's late and we're tired. What's the problem?"

She didn't want to, but at last she nodded. "Okay. I'm just too tired to go hunting for another room, and from the looks of it, everything is booked anyway. But that will mean you'll have to give me a ride back into town in the morning."

"I can do that." He was treading on dangerous ground once again and he knew it, as they headed toward his ranch. It couldn't be helped. It was nine-thirty and Bethany needed a place to stay. He had a guest house just sitting there. Tomorrow, after he took her back to town, he'd keep his distance.

The last place Bethany wanted to be was at Nate's ranch, but it had been the easiest solution to her problem. She didn't want to have to stay on the floor at her new place.

She remembered when his mother had fixed up the guest house years ago. She really liked his parents, his mom especially. They'd gotten along very well. Bethany asked about her, and she and Nate spent the twenty-minute drive talking about his parents and catching her up on what was happening in their lives. Finding out they spent most of their time in Florida these days, enjoying the sunshine, was a bit of a shock to her. Jared McMann taking it easy in Florida? No way! She couldn't imagine Nate's dad taking it easy—the man was a workaholic.

"It was a shock to me, too," Nate said. "But my mom always waited in the background, putting off things she wanted to do and see, while my dad worked here on the ranch. Dad said he realized when he woke up in the emergency room and looked at Mom that he owed her—that he'd been selfish all these years. So he stepped back and, believe it or not, he is enjoying himself. They travel some and come here a few times a year to see me. But Mom has really taken to the warmer weather and golf."

Wonders never ceased. She truly believed that Nate's dad would have died out there on a horse while working one day, and he would have been happy to go that way. He'd always been a nice man, but preoccupied with his work. Honestly, she wasn't sure whether he loved the ranch or loved the work. Nate loved the ranch. That had always been apparent.

"I'm glad your dad is enjoying life

a little—and realizing that your mom deserved more of his time."

"Yeah, you're right. A woman shouldn't have to give up everything for a man."

He didn't look at her when he said it, but Bethany wondered again if he might have believed this and told her he didn't love her so she could leave Treasure Creek in search of her career. It disturbed her again. She was lost in thought when he pulled the truck to a halt in front of the guest cabin.

"I always thought your mom liked the ranch. She and your dad always seemed to be happy."

Nate looked grave. "She did, but still—" he stopped midsentence. "Here we are. Let me carry your things in and then I'll get out of your hair. Make yourself at home," he said gruffly. "Sue is excited to know you're staying here tonight. She cooks breakfast at the big house about seven, if you want to come over."

He was ready to get away from her. That was apparent. "That sounds great," she said. She was happy he wasn't going to stick around. "I'll be ready, and then you can get me back to town if you don't mind. I'm anxious to start arranging the shop."

He seemed preoccupied, and barely looked at her as he carried her bags inside and then left. This was fine with her. She didn't want to spend any more time around him than she needed to. Especially tonight. There were so many unanswered questions crowding her brain, that all she wanted to do was take a long, hot shower, fall into bed and get a good night's sleep. Sleep would help her be able to focus. Time would help her figure out what questions she wanted or really needed answers to.

There was no forgetting watching the northern lights the night before. A lot had happened between then and now. It was hard to realize that that had been last night. But it had been. She needed sleep desperately because she hadn't gotten any then. She pushed the questions away, but they kept coming back—especially after the statement about his mom and dad. Would Nate have told her he didn't love her so that she could go to San Francisco in pursuit of her dream? Knowing what she'd just learned about his mom and dad, she wondered even more. She still didn't have an answer to how she felt about that, if it were true.

Bethany rose the next morning, dressed quickly and walked out onto the front porch of the small guest house. The sun was just peeking over the horizon as she leaned against the post to watch it. This was a beautiful place. The rolling pastures stretched wide and green with oats and rye. She'd ridden horseback many times with Nate to check on the cattle that roamed between the homestead and the mountains in the background. She'd dreamed of one day seeing her children riding horses here. Bethany stretched, leaning her head back to let the tension the thought brought her ease. She shouldn't have come here. The best thing to do was get the morning over with and head back to town.

"Bethany!" Sue Fowler exclaimed, throwing open the door and engulfing her in a tight hug as soon as Bethany knocked on it. "You are a sight for sore eyes."

"You are, too." Bethany returned the bear hug with one of her own. "You look wonderful."

"If you like plump and happy, that's me. Come, sit, sit," she said, ushering Bethany into the large kitchen. "Nate and Royce had to run off on ranch business. Nate asked me if I'd run you to town when we get through. I hope you don't mind."

She felt a mixture of relief and disappointment at the news. "Of course not. That would be great."

Suc had the omelets she was cooking on plates and in front of them within seconds. "So tell me about what's been going on with you and why you've decided to finally come home."

"The article brought me home."

Sue looked skeptical. "That is not the only reason. Tell me that you have finally realized what you've left behind."

"Actually, I have."

Sue's eyes widened. "I'm so happy. You

and Nate were always so perfect together. That boy needs you so much that I am just thankful that one of you has come to your senses."

Bethany's mouth fell open. "No. I mean I realized how much I missed *Treasure Creek* and all the people who live here. Like you and Royce. I didn't come back because of Nate."

Sue set her fork down. "And just why not?"

The question was so indignant that Bethany laughed. "Sue, I'm here to help other women plan their weddings."

"Well, I just don't know what to think about this," Sue said, huffing. "I just knew when I heard you were coming back that my prayers were answered. And then when you went on the tour with Nate, I thought everything was going to be like the old days. And then Royce said y'all were doing great when he brought the horses out."

Bethany was surprised by this information. "Why would you think such a thing,

Sue? You've been *praying* about this?" She was baffled.

"And why shouldn't I pray for Nate to find a good woman and settle down? The man needs to do that, and soon. He's not getting any younger. It's been ten years since you left."

It was a fair question and a good reason, Bethany thought. So why did Sue blush slightly? Had she said something she didn't mean to say?

"If you didn't come back for Nate, then I guess I'll just have to pray something changes your mind and the both of you get some sense. And soon."

Before going into her shop, Bethany stopped by the tour company to see Amy.

"Bethany! Are you okay?" Rachel, the receptionist, exclaimed, the instant she walked through the door. She'd been in conversation with Delilah, the woman who'd come into the shop and told Bethany she was going to be married by Christmas.

The woman wore a big, furry, black parka that made her look like she'd climbed into a gorilla suit. The matching black, furry ski boots were actually an improvement over the black, spiky-heeled ones she'd had on when Bethany first met her.

"I can't imagine how horrible it was finding this dead man. Tucker Lawson, isn't that his name?"

Bethany was startled. "Did they ID him?" She'd thought it would take a little longer than a few hours.

"No," Rachel was quick to interject. "Gage came by on his way over to the sheriff's office and said it was too soon." She was standing behind Delilah and shot Bethany a look of exasperation aimed at the newcomer.

Delilah placed a dramatic hand over her heart. "You aren't telling me that running across dead bodies is common around here, are you? I mean, really—from what I've heard, this Tucker guy had a plane crash. Aren't they still conducting a search for the plane?"

"No," Bethany explained patiently. "Reed said they would begin an extensive search the minute they knew whose body we found."

"Perfect. I just booked a day trip for tomorrow with that handsome Morgan Todd." She gave Bethany a knowing look. "I'm hopping a blizzard strikes and we have to hole up in a miner's cabin. If I'd have known about the tour you just went on with that handsome hunk of cowboy, Nate McMann, I would have signed up for that. Now *there's* a man. I just can't figure out how to get him to notice me. I don't really know what to think about these rugged types. I just can't seem to do anything right to get their attention. Hopefully, tomorrow my luck shall change."

Bethany didn't exactly know what to say about that. Yes, Nate was most definitely a man—and she was pretty sure that he'd noticed Delilah. How could he not? How could anyone not notice her? Catching sight of Amy at the end of the room, past all of the cubicles, she started to head that way. "I hope you have fun on your tour tomorrow. And I'll be in the shop for our appointment on Thursday, if you still want to come by."

"I wouldn't miss it for the world. Who knows? I might even have a prospect by tomorrow." Winking, she waved her bejeweled fingers and sashayed toward the door, gorilla hair swinging in all directions with each swaying step. No sooner had she left the building, when suddenly, men came from everywhere. Only then did Bethany realize exactly how few people had been in the room when Delilah was there.

"I can't believe you booked me with her!" Morgan Todd came marching from the broom closet—a scowl wreaking havoc on his rugged face. He was in his midthirties, and not one of the guys she'd known when she lived here. Though he'd driven them in last night, she'd been visiting with Shelly, Robert and Cody, and had left him and Nate to sit up front in the van.

Another cute guy, a thin fellow with an engaging smile and a faint scar on his face, looked relieved. He'd edged out of the break room after making certain the coast was clear. "Better you than me. That woman scares me."

"Ethan, that might just be your woman right there," Rachel said, teasing. "You'd better be glad you have to teach school, or I might have talked her into a trip with you, too. You both know she needs a husband by Christmas, and I think one of you should step up and accommodate her."

"Not me," Ethan said.

"Your gonna have some payback comin' from me," Morgan said to Rachel, a teasing, half serious glint in his eyes.

Bethany laughed and headed toward Amy. It was nice to know life in the tour company was still upbeat and fun. That was the way it had been when she was a part of it.

"Thanks for coming by," Amy said. "Come in the office and give me your version of the story. I am so sorry this happened on your first tour back. Are you okay? It didn't upset you too bad, did it? It's just a horrible thing."

"I'm fine. Really," Bethany said, taking a

seat across from Amy as she plunked down behind the desk and let out a sigh. "I hated that we found this poor man, but at least we've found him. And now, whoever he is, he's not out there forgotten. His family can be notified if they've been searching for him."

"That's what I'm thinking, too. Glad you're looking at it that way."

Bethany realized Amy was pale. "Are you all right?"

Amy took a breath and confessed, "Not really. Its just that I have a lot on my mind, and this has just brought back memories of Ben's death. It's hard."

"I'm so sorry. I know it can't be easy."

"No. And on top of that I got another wedding proposal this morning, from some man over the phone." She made a strangled sound of frustration. "I mean, it's one thing to get them from the guys here in town who think they are helping, but it's an entirely different thing to get them from strangers looking to make a buck on the treasure!"

The very idea had Bethany's dander up.

"I hope you hung up on the creep. That really burns my bacon."

Amy chuckled. "Actually, I told him no, then hung up on him. Anyway, on to more important things… What about you and Nate? How did you get along?"

"That depends on which moment we're talking about. We were civil one moment, and not the next."

Amy brightened. "That sounds promising to me. A few sparks never hurt any relationship."

"*Amy*—"

"*Bethany,* that man may have told you he didn't love you, but you and I both know deep down that he did. I for one can't figure out why he would do such a thing."

Bethany toyed with the idea of telling her what she thought he might have been thinking, but that would mean exposing to Amy that she wanted a new romance with him.

"If you figure it out let me know, but I've moved on with my life, Amy. Ben is trying to help you move on with your life. Yes, I was crazy in love with Nate—until he broke my heart. I moved away and had to force myself to move forward. It's not easy, but it's the healthy thing to do." They stared at each other for a moment.

"I didn't mean to cause you pain with all of this," Amy said at last. "But you're right. I guess I got caught up in the idea that while I can't have Ben back, there is still a chance for you and Nate. Forgive me. I wasn't thinking about how hard that might be on you."

"If there is one thing I've learned, it's that I can deal with more than I ever thought possible."

"God is good to stand beside us, isn't He?"

Bethany thought about that. On the hike she'd begun to pray more, and she had started trying to rebuild her relationship with God. She thought about what Shelly said about God's timing in her life, and the way everything worked out so perfectly.

"Yes, that's true," she said, trying to see it through Amy's eyes. "Well, I have to go to the shop. I have a lot to get set up and I have to run over to the hotel and see about a room."

"I thought you had one."

She quickly told her what had happened.

"Oh, I see. You're more than welcome to stay at my house. I have an extra room."

The offer made Bethany feel good. "Thank you so much. They said I'd have one tonight, so I'm not worried."

"I just had an idea. I'm getting together several ladies to help make costumes for the Christmas pageant. Would you be interested in helping out with that?"

Bethany didn't hesitate. "Sure. That sounds like fun—just don't ask me to sing."

Amy laughed. "That was my next question. But at this point, it's more your talent for sewing that I'm looking for than your singing ability. It is amazing how many people can't sew these days."

"In my case, it's the can't sing that's appropriate. Look, I'd better run. I have furniture to move and boxes to unload. Will you let me know when you hear something about the body?"

"Do you need some help?"

"I think I've got it. The movers will place the big things, but if I need you I'll holler."

"Okay, and I will let you and everyone know as soon as we hear back on the identity. Thanks again for coming to my rescue on this tour. Everyone had only high praises for you. Shelly said Cody loved you to death and that you made a lifelong impression on him."

Bethany left the tour company with a spring in her step, thinking about Cody. It felt good to know that she'd touched Cody's young life in a positive way. There had been a time when she wouldn't have considered adoption. It was something people who couldn't have their own children did. She'd never really thought about it as an option. But as she entered her shop, the idea weighed heavy on her heart.

Chapter Thirteen

Nate hated leaving the house before saying goodbye to Bethany. He and Royce had to check on a load of cattle that was supposed to be shipped, and there was a conflict that he had to rectify.

A little before noon, he watched the semi full of cattle pull out, headed for the border. "Glad that's done," he snapped, then turning, he stalked into the office. Inside, he slammed the drawer to the file cabinet shut then slumped into his chair behind his desk. This had been his father's desk and his grandfather's before that. The office was small for the operation they ran, but held such sentimental value that Nate hadn't ever wanted to enlarge the space. Decorated with Alaskan carvings and cattle hides, the room usually gave him at least a semblance of peace.

Not today. He turned his chair to the window and scowled at the sweeping vista before him. The same view his dad and grandfather had studied. He'd hoped to pass this on to his son one day. Only, there wouldn't be one for him. The buck stopped here.

"What's wrong with you?" Royce asked, stomping into the office. "You've been in a foul mood from the moment you woke up this morning."

"A man has a right to a foul mood if he wants it," Nate grunted.

"I reckon that's right, but you take that attitude back home and show it to Sue, and you'll get more questions than you want. I can guarantee it. This is about Bethany, isn't it?"

Nate turned his chair halfway around and glanced sideways at his old friend. Royce knew the truth when no one else did. He'd come up on Nate back behind the barn, right after he'd told Bethany he didn't love her. Royce had seen the way it had torn his heart out to lie to her like that—to see the pain in her face and the betrayal. He'd been so upset that he'd blurted out to Royce what he'd done and why; and to his surprise, Royce had told him to go after her. When he hadn't, Royce had kept his secret, even from his parents and Sue. And after a few times of trying to convince him to go after her, he'd respected Nate's choice and stopped talking about it.

"I don't know what I'm supposed to do, Royce. She's here, and she still is affected by what I did to her."

"She's not the only one. Son, you've never been the same since that day. Everyone can see it. They may not know what it is that broke you and Bethany up, but they know that the day she left you shut down a part of yourself that ain't never been opened up again. I thought your spending time with her out there would be a good thing."

Nate grunted again. "She tolerated me.

She hasn't ever forgiven me for betraying her like I did."

"You need to come clean with her. Tell her you love her but you can't give her kids. Like I said before, she'll be fine with it…if she still loves you."

Nate shook his head. "I let her go to pursue her dreams—"

"And those dreams have brought her right back here, where she belongs. So what are you waiting on? The Lord is giving you a second chance to set things right."

He hadn't thought about it that way. "I don't think so. When she finds out I lied to her, she'll never forgive me. Never trust me."

"Love can forgive a lot."

Nate wasn't so sure of that. He'd been thinking long and hard about what he'd done. He didn't think he could ask her to do such a thing. But he couldn't stop thinking about her, either.

"You got it from here?" he asked, standing and heading to the door.

"I do. You headed to town?"

"Yup."

"Give that little gal my best, and my rec-ommendation is like it always has been. Tell her the truth. Put a little faith in the fact that she can make the right decision, given all the facts. A woman has the right to her own mind. I've stayed out of it because I'm your friend, and I'll go to my grave with what I know if that's the way you want it. But that ain't saying I agree. You did what you thought was right because you loved her. But the truth is always the best route. Like the Good Book says, the truth will set you free."

"I'm not going to see Bethany. I've got a staff meeting at the tour company."

Royce followed him outside, tucked his fingers into his pockets and rocked back on his heels. "Tell Bethany hello for me."

"I'm not going by there, Royce."

"Look, all I'm sayin' is don't shut her out. Go see her. Talk to her—about anything."

"That's not going to help."

"Nate, you can't go through life living a lie."

* * *

"Well, hi, honey," Joleen Jones said, just before lunch.

Bethany had been sorting things in her shop—in between dealing with curious women peeking in to see if she was open for business yet. Goodness, but the ladies were "chompin' at the bit to get married," as her daddy was fond of saying. She'd decided to take a break and head over to Lizbet's for a hamburger and maybe a milkshake. She was still debating this issue when she turned the corner and literally ran into Joleen.

"What are you doing? Are you all right?" If Bethany was seeing things right Joleen had been hovering at the edge of The General Store, peeking inside.

Joleen waved a hand of dismissal. "I'm fine. Really, I am. Are *you?* I guess I shouldn't have been in your way." She leaned forward and whispered, "I hope you know I haven't told anyone that I'm planning on marrying Harry. He—well, it just would seem a bit odd if I started spouting that sort of thing. Don't you think?"

She was so cute, Bethany thought. And sweet…but yes, if she started telling the world her plan to marry Harry, others might think there was a screw loose or something. Then again, Delilah was telling the world that she'd made a bet with one of her male friends, that if she wasn't married by the time she was thirty that she would marry him. Bethany had heard the entire story from Sue that morning on the way into town. Apparently, Delilah was not afraid to tell her story to anyone who would listen.

Poor Morgan. Bethany would like to be a fly on that wall tomorrow. Of course, no one took her seriously. And no one would take Joleen seriously, either. Especially Harry.

"What are you doing out here?"

"Oh, nothing. I…well…" Joleen blushed. "I have been in there four times already. I've been trying to get up the courage to ask Harry out to dinner. And well, he just keeps—well, he is just so cute, and I can't get up the nerve to do it."

Cute. Joleen had called Harry cute!

Bethany glanced in the window at the proprietor. If he didn't look so blah, maybe had a little life in his round face, maybe he could be considered cute. Well, *kind* of cute.

"Would you go in and help me?"

Bethany blinked in dismay. "Help you?"

Joleen smiled a hesitant but hopeful smile. "Yes, you go in ahead of me. Then I'll go in, and if I can't ask him, you can maybe stand to the side and prod me on. You know, like they do in the movies? Be my rooting section."

Bethany had just said she'd like to be a fly on the wall, and now she was being asked to be one. But no. She couldn't do this. Joleen's smile faded and her big honey eyes misted.

"Sure, I can do that." Bethany would have kicked herself if she could have twisted around enough. Of all the crazy things to do. Talk about unprofessional!

"Oh, honey, I just knew you wouldn't let me down. Okay, you go first. Don't let him know you know me. I mean, does that sound like the best thing?"

"Whatever you think."

Joleen nodded. "I think that's right. I can do this. There is no law that says a woman can't ask a man on a date. She can even ask him to marry her—"

"Wait, maybe you should just stick with asking him for the date."

Breathing nervously, Joleen nodded. "Right. That's what I'll do. Okay, go."

Bethany walked into the store. There were a few people milling around up front. Harry was helping an older man pick out a pair of socks. "Good afternoon," he said, when she entered.

"Hello," she said. "I'm just going to check out, um, the preserves." Not exactly sure how to handle herself in this situation, Bethany moved to stand next to the canned goods. She studied them intently, watching the door out of the corner of her eye. From where she was standing she could see Harry's profile.

The older man was holding up two black

socks. "All I'm sayin' is, do you think this length is the one I should get, or this length?" he asked, holding up first one sock and then the other. Harry studied them intently.

"Personally, Mr. Billerbeck, the longer one—" he halted talking as Joleen moved into the store. And *moved into* was the term. The woman flitted in like a butterfly. She stopped at first one bin and then the next. Dramatically, she picked up a package of batteries and studied them as though they were gold. And then she slid a sideways glance Harry's way. Instantly, Harry started talking about socks again. "Short, I mean, long socks is what I wear."

Bethany dropped the can of peaches she was holding. It crashed to the floor and all eyes turned her way. "Sorry," she said, and went to look for the can as it rolled down the aisle.

"Looking for this?" Nate was standing behind the toothpaste, holding her can of peaches.

"Yes, thank you." She was embarrassed

and took the can, glancing over her shoulder to see what was going on.

"What are you doing?" he asked. "I've been standing here watching you, and it looks like you're watching Harry on a covert op. *Are* you watching Harry?"

"No!" she hissed. "I'm not—well, I mean I am. But…"

Nate hitched a brow and his lip twitched. He leaned around so he could see better. "Are you trying to figure out if you want the long black sock or the short black sock?"

The man was too funny. She frowned. "I am not buying socks, and you know it." Joleen had moved closer to Harry and was looking about, trying to locate Bethany—who leaned around the mouthwash section just enough for Joleen to see her. "Go," she mouthed to the woman. "Ask him."

"You're coaching that woman," Nate whispered indignantly. His breath was warm and tingled all the way to her toes.

Bethany almost forgot what she was doing. "Be quiet," she whispered, glaring at him. His blue eyes twinkled, and she forgot to breathe.

"You're coaching that Joleen woman on how to do something—"

"Don't you have somewhere you need to be?"

"Nope. I'm fine right here. My curiosity is getting the better of me. You know she was dating some leech last month. I think someone said she was trying to make ole Harry jealous."

Bethany told herself to take a breath and look away from the blue eyes. She was proud of herself when she broke contact. His comment was new to her. Joleen had a bottle of pickled eggs and was carrying them to the counter. Harry excused himself from explaining about the socks and hurried to the counter. His face was a blank canvas, though, none of the interest Bethany had seen on his profile when Joleen had entered the building showed now.

Bethany couldn't move. She had Nate breathing down her neck on one side, and a row of moon pies in her way on the other side. Joleen was nervous as she set the pickled eggs on the counter and smiled at Harry.

He swiped at his hair and straightened. "Is that all?" he asked in his most dire, almost disapproving voice. It sounded like he was telling her that her cat had just died, and it was her fault.

"Y-yes, I think that should do it."

"You like pickled eggs?"

"No. I mean yes. I love them."

"*Oh, brother,*" Bethany groaned under her breath. "Just ask the man already!"

Nate chuckled in her ear. "Is she trying to ask Harry out?"

Bethany hadn't meant to say that out loud.

"She is, isn't she?"

"And what if she is?"

Nate grinned. "Hey, I think that's great. Look at the man—he *needs* someone to ask him out."

But Joleen didn't. She glanced around, didn't see Bethany behind the moon pies or mouthwash, grabbed her bag the moment

Harry packed up the gallon jug of eggs and hurried from the store before he could give her her change. Harry leaned out over the counter, holding out a handful of change, and watched her go.

The man was interested in her. There was no doubt about it.

Nate shook his head. "Boy, those two need help."

Bethany agreed. She was worried about Joleen. "I need to go." She scooted past him and hurried outside. She stared down the sidewalk, but Joleen was nowhere in sight. Where could she have gone? Feeling bad for the sweet woman, she started walking down the sidewalk in search of her. Nate fell into step with her.

"Are you looking for her?"

"Yes, she's really sweet."

"From what I hear, she's been trying to get his attention for some time now. But I don't think the man knows *how* to ask someone out."

"Didn't someone break his heart when we

were in high school? I seem to remember something about that."

"Yeah, my parents talked about it. He fell head over heels for this gal—a real gold digger, my dad called her. When she left town, it pretty much tore him up."

Bethany felt for the grumpy man. She could honestly say she empathized with him. "Joleen might be good for him." She glanced down the next side street and stopped. "I don't see her anywhere, and I know she was upset."

"That was obvious—even to Harry."

"Do you think that's why Harry almost broke his neck watching her when she left? Or do you think he was wishing he'd at least asked her about more than her pickled eggs?"

Nate chuckled. The sound gave Bethany a warm, fuzzy feeling, even as worried about Joleen as she was.

"I'm pretty sure he wishes that he'd talked to her more. He was so lost in thought when I followed you out that the sock guy couldn't get a response out of him. Not even when he waved his socks in Harry's face and demanded attention."

Bethany laughed. "I hope Joleen is all right. She wants…" she stopped. She couldn't tell him that Joleen was talking marriage. "She seems like she really wants to go out with him."

"I'd say you're right on the money with that one," Nate drawled. "But it might take some help from outside."

They'd started walking again, and Bethany turned abruptly to Nate. "Do you think you could help make that happen?" she asked, feeling optimistic.

Nate pushed his hat back with his thumb, as a slow, cocky smile spread across his ruggedly handsome face. "I can sure give it a shot, if that's what you want me to do."

Despite the alarm bells clanging in her head, Bethany could have kissed him for that—she *didn't*—*but she could have*.

Chapter Fourteen

"So, any news on the body?" Ethan Eckles, a school teacher who led a few tours a month, asked, as soon as Nate and Gage entered the staff meeting.

After not finding Joleen, Nate had left Bethany at her shop and rushed over to get to the meeting. He met Gage hurrying inside the building, but they were both running late, so he didn't have time to ask if he'd heard anything. "I don't know. Have you heard anything, Gage?"

Gage shook his head just as Amy walked in, sat and took her post at the front of the room. "There is no news yet," she said. "I just talked to Reed."

"Jake is really having faith that it isn't Tucker," Casey Donner said. Casey's fiancé, Jake Rodgers, had gone to school with him and was Tucker's best friend. He hadn't given up on his friend and was still searching for him.

Nate never figured Tucker for a guy who would run from life. But that was exactly what it seemed like. He and his dad hadn't gotten along for years. Tucker had come home after his dad's death and had been angry that, even knowing he was dying, his dad hadn't reached out to him…hadn't tried to straighten out the problems between them. It bothered Nate to think that Tucker and his dad could both die distant like that. All it would have taken for them to begin the road to reconciliation was for the two of them to sit down in an open and honest conversation.

"I'm praying it isn't Tucker, too," Amy said. "But Reed warned me not to get my hopes up, so I'm going to pass that on to all of you who knew Tucker. We don't want it to be him, but it very well may be. Reed will let us know just as soon as he hears anything.

"As most of you know, Nate didn't have any luck with the clues on the map, either. So everyone needs to continue to keep their eyes open. Think hard, and if any of you think of any places that you've been that might be a likely place Mack may have thought to hide it, let's explore it."

Nate listened to the rest of the meeting, but his thoughts kept going back to Bethany. He'd toyed with the idea of stopping by to see her all the way into town. Sure, he'd told Royce that he wasn't, but that didn't mean he hadn't thought about it.

Royce had been a good friend all these years, keeping his secret and respecting Nate's choice, while at the same time giving his honest opinion—which was that he believed Nate had made the wrong choice. Nate hadn't thought so. But on the tour this last week, things weren't looking so clear any more. The fact that he'd lied bothered him more and more every day. Trying to justify that he was doing the right thing for Bethany was starting to weigh heavy on his conscience, and it was not cutting it any longer.

Again, the questions kept coming back to him: had he taken the easy road out by not telling Bethany he couldn't have children? Should he have given her the option of making up her own mind, given the facts? Even at the risk of her choosing to stay with him out of pity—or leave him out of disappointment.

Honest conversation.

The Lord didn't take to lying. Nate rubbed his temple, trying to ease the tension building up behind his eyes. When the meeting was over, he told everyone goodbye and headed straight for his truck. He didn't want to talk to anyone. But spying the moving van across the way, in front of Bethany's shop, he knew he had to go see if she needed him.

He was about to start across the street, when a couple of women rounded the corner and headed inside her shop. One of them was that Delilah woman. Nate cringed. The two moving men almost dropped Bethany's red couch as Delilah and her other fancy friend sashayed past them. Spinning on the heel of his cowboy boot, Nate made fast tracks back to his truck. No way was he going over there now. Besides, Bethany had a business to run. She had moving men there to unload her things, so there was really no reason for him to stop by.

Climbing into his truck, he headed toward home. He'd heard Morgan complaining that he was going to have to take Delilah on a tour tomorrow. Poor guy. Nate felt for him.

Although, the one positive was that seeing Delilah had stopped him from making a mistake. He had to keep his distance. There were times when there would be no way to avoid Bethany; but then there were other times, like just now, where he'd been about to seek her out—and those were avoidable. He had to remember that.

And he had to get his head on straight, get all this crazy stuff batting around inside it figured out and under control before he saw her again. If not, he might make a mistake and say something he didn't need to say.

And more important, something Bethany didn't need to hear.

He was halfway home when he remembered he'd promised to see if he could encourage Harry to ask Joleen out. He made a mental note to do that the next time he was in town. He'd promised Bethany he'd do it, and he was going to make good on that promise if it was the last thing he did.

Bethany had so much on her mind that she was having trouble thinking straight. After Nate had tried to help her find Joleen the day before, she'd thrown herself into setting up her shop. And since her furniture and things had arrived, she was able to get started a little on setting things up in the apartment above the shop. She stayed working late into the night, but opted not to spend the night there yet. It was still too disheveled. A big mess was what it was, but she was making progress. Still, though, as she finally headed back to the hotel, she felt distracted, partly, to a small degree, from thinking about Joleen. Where had she gone? She wasn't the woman's keeper, but she was really worried about her.

Then there was Nate. Pushing furniture around and arranging displays didn't distract her from thinking about him. She'd still not approached him about why he had told her he didn't love her. Was she chicken?

She decided that the answer was a resounding *yes!*

How could it be that after all these years she could still feel like he was the right man for her? Oh, she'd tried to deny it. Tried so hard it hurt. But when he offered to help her look for Joleen she'd been so happy to have him beside her. And in the store, he'd almost driven her crazy with his nearness. They needed to have a talk. A long talk.

But she'd known it wasn't the time. Not when she had so many things to do and she was still so mixed up.

When she couldn't sleep, she crawled out of bed and sat at the window of the hotel room, staring out over the town. Down the road, across the street, she could see the church. It stood out in the dark, illuminated by the street lamps. She'd been in Treasure Creek almost two weeks. Maybe Sunday she would go. It was Friday, and she had the overwhelming urge to dress and go there now. Rubbing her hand over her eyes, she found herself praying automatically for God to help her find peace. For God to lead her.

She rose from her chair and went to the hotel dresser and found the Bible—her own was packed away somewhere in all the boxes at her shop.

Settling back in her seat at the window, Bethany took a deep breath and then opened the Bible and began to read. She opened it automatically to "Psalms," but then she stopped reading the passage and flipped pages. Stopping finally, her gaze landed on the passage that seemed to be calling to her. It was *Romans* 15:13. She read it silently and then she reread it out loud in the quietness of her empty room.

"May the God of hope fill you with all joy and peace as you trust in Him, so that you may overflow with hope by the power of the Holy Spirit." Her soft words seemed to echo in the room.

She closed her eyes. "Please, Lord," she prayed. "Bring me back to You and let me feel that peace again. Let me know You are here and leading me."

She opened her eyes. "I trust You."

The last three words were hard to say. It had been a long, long time since she'd trusted anyone. Especially God. Maybe she could do it.

"Hi, Harry," Bethany said, the next morning as she walked in to grab some staples and tape. The day was beautiful, the sky was clear and endlessly blue and Bethany just felt good. Harry glanced up from ringing up a purchase and gave her a nod. Not a happy nod, but what else did she expect from the grumpy man? Boy, did he ever need Joleen to lighten up his world!

Not exactly sure where the staples were in the jam-packed store, she wandered down the rows, keeping a sharp eye out for them. She finally found them at the back and headed up front. She felt better today, hopeful beyond belief that if she put her trust in God, He would help her figure out her life.

"I need supplies for a trip into the wilderness," a pretty woman was telling Harry, as Bethany reached the counter.

"Are you planning on a day trip or a week-long trip?"

The woman had beautiful, long blond hair that looked even longer because she was so tall and willowy. She stared blankly at Harry with her blue eyes, making it apparent to all who were listening that she hadn't a clue about camping. This was obviously nothing new to Harry, and two older men, who were standing beside the fishing tackle on the front wall, were gawking at her. She wore a white parka, a bright pink cap and fur boots—much the same outfit as many of the women who'd come to town with the intention of hooking themselves a hunky tour guide.

Realizing Harry was going to be a while, Bethany decided to find a card from the small rack beside the counter. Though she'd called her parents after she arrived, she thought they would enjoy a scenic card from Alaska.

With a scowl, Harry headed toward the backpacks at the rear of the room, all the while trying to explain to the woman, who looked vaguely familiar to Bethany, how the compass she was holding out to him worked.

"That's that Penelope Lear," one of the old men leaned over and said to the other one. His voice carried. "You know, of the Alaskan Lears?"

Bethany did a double take. Everyone in Alaska knew who the Lears were. They were basically the most prominent family in Alaska. Now she realized why the woman had looked familiar, her photograph made the society pages often. Hiking in the wilderness totally did not fit her profile.

"Yup, you should have seen the jet she flew in on. And them suitcases—it should'a took a Seven-Forty-Seven just ta fly all them bags in."

"Harry better send her straight over to Alaska's Treasures tours company instead of selling her a compass," the second old man said, chuckling, as the two stepped outside and headed down the sidewalk. "I don't know why she's come to Treasure Creek, with all them fancy city slickers she's always in the papers with…." their voices faded away as the door closed behind them.

"So I need jerky, a backpack, water— what else," Penelope asked. Bethany tried not to eavesdrop, but it was hard, since they'd moved to the counter and unloaded all the stuff. Harry looked at the things and grinned at Penelope—actually grinned. But then he suddenly swiped his hand over his hair and stuck his shoulders back. Bethany realized, the same instant that Penelope did, that he was watching Joleen enter the store.

"Joleen!" Bethany called, hurrying over to give her a quick hug. She couldn't help herself. "How are you," she whispered.

Joleen smiled sweetly and gave her a wink. Then they turned away from the rest of the store to talk privately in hushed tones. "I'm just fine. I was just in a sad mood yesterday. You ever get to feeling blue like that? You know, when you don't think things are ever going to go your way?"

Bethany smiled, she couldn't help it. Joleen was a breath of fresh air beneath all that hair and makeup. "Yes, I do."

"Well, that's what happened to me. I'm sorry I rushed out of here like a crazy woman. I just got the jitters. And, honey, I saw that cute hunk of a cowboy flirting with you and thought you didn't need to be worrying about me."

"Oh, he wasn't flirting with me. I was trying to do what you wanted. I just—"

"Oh, you don't owe me any explanations. I just realized, standing there, that I was in no mood to try to ask Harry out, so that's why I hurried out of here. I went on back to my room and gave myself a good talking to. I realized I didn't need to be asking that man out. I'm a little old-fashioned for that, and so, I'll just stick to my guns. I know that man is crazy about me…he gets jealous, too. A man doesn't get jealous if he doesn't care. So I fixed myself up last night and went over to the singles' mingle and had myself a great time."

"The singles' mingle?"

Joleen chuckled. "That's what I call it when the singles get together over at the church."

"Ohhh."

"You should come with me next time— though, with the way that Nate McMann was hanging around, I don't think you need to. Did he ask you out?"

How had it gone from talking about Joleen to talking about Nate? "No. He didn't—wouldn't."

"And why not?"

"Well, because, well…I don't want him

to." Bethany glanced up as Penelope passed by with her bags in hand. She gave them a hesitant smile before heading out the door.

"You know that is not true." Joleen placed a red-tipped fingernail against her chin and studied her. "I saw the way you looked at him yesterday. I tell you what, next week you are coming to the singles' mingle with me. Maybe Nate will be there. Some of his friends come. Harry was there last night," she whispered the last part and looked over Bethany's shoulder. "Hi, Harry," she said, turning up the volume on her smile. "I sure had fun last night. Didn't you?"

Harry looked sheepish. "I did." He looked at Bethany. "Do you want me to ring those up for you?" He glanced at Joleen.

Joleen gave him her big smile.

It didn't take much for Bethany to realize she needed to hit the road. "That would be great," she said.

"What?" Harry asked, distracted by the blinding display of pearly whites Joleen was flashing him.

"If you let me pay."

"Oh, right," Harry said, snapping to, and practically snatching her things out of her arms. Within seconds, Bethany was paid up, and he practically ushered her out. Smiling, she waved at Joleen and said a prayer that things were about to go her way.

Chapter Fifteen

Bethany went to church on Sunday. It was a good day. She was approached by Casey Donner and her fiancé, Jake Rodgers, both of whom she'd known in school. Casey asked if she would help plan their wedding which was that month, and she agreed. Bethany thought they were a great couple, and it was so nice to see how Jake's teenage daughter and Casey got along. It was obvious they loved each other; Bethany was reminded again that adopting a child was an option for her.

It was as if God was pushing home a point when Gage Parker introduced her to his new wife, Karenna. She was holding his brother's baby and it was obvious she loved and adored her new nephew. Bethany held little Matthew, and a longing so strong she could barely stand it came over her.

She sat with Amy and her boys, Dexter and Sammy. When Bethany looked at them she saw Ben, and her heart ached for Amy. But at the same time, she knew that these two darling boys were gifts of love, blessings from the Lord for Amy.

When the service started, Bethany was disappointed when she looked about and didn't see Nate. She listened as Pastor Michaels gave a sermon based on the verse *1 Thessalonians* 5:18—"Give thanks in all circumstances, for this is God's will for you in Christ Jesus."

He pointed out that the verse didn't say, give thanks *for* all circumstances, but *in* all circumstances. A reminder from the Lord that, even when circumstances were not to our liking, we were still supposed to give thanks to God and trust Him.

Trust Him.

When the sermon was over, she had

barely stood up when someone touched her shoulder. Turning, she found herself looking up into Nate's blue eyes. Instantly, her heart faltered, dropping with the speed of a diving eagle—then, like the eagle spreading its wings and catching wind, it soared. She swallowed and tried hard to hide the silly grin that instantaneously sprang to her lips.

"Hello," he said. He was holding his hat in his hand, it rested across his heart leaving him with a mat of pressed blond hat hair.

"I didn't think you were here."

His eyes brightened. "I slipped in the back during the first song. It was a good sermon."

She nodded.

Amy gave him a hug. "Hi, Nate. It's good to see you here."

"Hey, Nate," Dexter said. "See my buckle?"

"Mine, too," Sammy said, echoing his big brother. Both boys leaned back awkwardly to show Nate their new silver buckles.

Nate dropped to one knee, reaching out to touch the gold bucking bull on Dexter's buckle. "Oh, doggy, but those are some cool lookin' buckles, buckaroos. You win those riding bulls?"

"Nope," Dexter quipped, while Sammy wagged his head from side to side. "But when I do, you can come watch me."

Nate chuckled. "I'll do that," he promised, then stood up. "Bethany, have you made any lunch plans?"

"Now she has—with you," Amy smiled. "Come on, boys, let's head home. It's lunchtime for you, too."

"So, did you?" Nate asked, as soon as Amy was gone. The church had cleared out and they were the only ones left in the sanctuary.

Bethany took a few moments to calm her racing heart. "According to Amy, I do." That got her that slow smile that tended to curl her toes every time.

"But what about according to you? I really would like to talk. I think we need to."

"Yes, we do."

* * *

They chose Martelli's. By the time they got to the table, they'd visited with over half a dozen people who had also gone there to eat after church.

Nate wanted to come clean with Bethany, but the place was too crowded for what he needed to tell her.

"So, how's everything going?" he asked, when they finally got shown to their seats. They were in a bad spot, probably the worst seat in the house, since it was the table that sat at the front of the restaurant, near the entrance. They were basically on display. Both of them were very aware of the fact.

"I'm getting booked quickly. Casey and Jake even hired me."

"Hey, that's great."

The waitress took their order. They both ordered the special of the day, sirloin and grilled vegetables. Nate didn't know if Bethany felt the same way as he did, but it didn't really matter what they ate. He wasn't going to taste any of it.

"Have you heard anything from Reed?" Bethany asked, after a dead silence stretched between them.

"Not yet," Nate said, glad she'd asked. "But this next week we're sure to hear something. I spoke to Jake this morning."

"Good. It will be good to finally know. I talked to Shelly yesterday. They are home, and had pictures developed, and couldn't get over how beautiful the trip was. They wondered about the man's identity, too."

"They were a neat couple. I keep thinking about Cody."

"Me, too." Bethany looked troubled.

"Is something wrong?"

"No—I thought the sermon was great today. I needed to hear what the pastor had to say. I think people who adopt children are wonderful. I'm thinking I might—"

"What?" he asked, when she cut off mid-sentence.

"Nothing," she said, as their food arrived.

Before he could coax her to continue, people who had finished eating began leaving slowly, in what seemed like timed intervals, each one stopped by their table to talk before they left. Bethany smiled and laughed and enjoyed visiting with everyone she hadn't seen in years. She never tried to finish what she was about to say.

When the meal was finally over, Nate was about as frustrated as a trapped bear. He'd started out to tell Bethany the truth about their past. But he should have taken her somewhere quiet. He *needed* to tell her the truth. But had she been about to tell him she was thinking about adopting? He needed that question answered. He needed to come right out and ask it. But would that make a difference for him now?

She was looking as beautiful to him as always, and sitting across from her, he saw her as he'd always dreamed of her—his wife.

They finally walked outside. The day had turned overcast and the wind had picked up. In the distance, the mountains were a mere shadow through the heavy mist hovering around them. The weight about Nate's heart felt heavy.

"Nate," she asked, when they reached her shop, "what's on your mind?"

Bethany had always been able to tell when something was bothering him. "I need to confess something to you. But out here isn't the place."

"Then come inside."

He waited as she opened the door, and then stepped into her shop. Glancing about the room filled with wedding photos, china displays, flower displays and all manner of wedding paraphernalia that made dream weddings into reality, he instantly wished he'd gone home.

"I can't have children, Bethany." There was no use not cutting to the core. It needed to be said, and if he'd tried any other way, he might not have gotten it out.

Bethany had her back to him, and she slowly set her purse on the table and turned. "I'm so sorry. When did you find this out?"

Nate yanked his hat off. It was time.

"I learned about this the day before graduation."

Bethany inhaled sharply. "What are you telling me?"

"I couldn't let you stay. Not when you had such big dreams. Not when I couldn't give you the children you wanted." He didn't need to fill in all the spaces, say it word-for-word. Her expression said it all.

"So you lied to me to make me leave? You told me you didn't love me."

He wanted to reach out to her—wanted to tell her he still loved her, but what difference would it make?"

"I was wrong to lie to you. In my heart I thought I was doing what was right for you. I couldn't have you marrying me when you knew I could never give you all those babies you wanted. I didn't want you confused. You were young. You might have married me, given up your career and your dream of children, and I couldn't live with that."

"So you made the decision for me," she said flatly. "All these years apart have been based on a lie."

"Yes. I hope you can forgive me."

"I think you should leave." She walked to the door and opened it. "There's nothing to forgive Nate. You didn't lie, as far as I can see. You didn't tell me you couldn't have children, and that's your business. What you told me instead was that you didn't love me. And I don't think that was a lie either. If you *had* loved me, you would have trusted me enough to make my own decision about what was right for me."

"Going to follow your dreams was right for you."

She shook her head. "So why are you telling me this now?"

"Because it's the right thing to do. I realized it when we were on the trail." He could tell it was hitting her hard. She was too calm.

"Well, thank you." She opened the door wide, his signal to exit.

Her eyes were wounded, yet she was trying to hide it by holding her chin up. But her hand shook as she reached for the doorknob. He still couldn't tell what she was thinking. He should say something, but what? In the end, he decided the best thing was to leave and let her digest what he'd just told her.

If she was going to hate him, then so be it. All he could hope was that she might eventually forgive him.

Chapter Sixteen

After Nate left, Bethany locked up the shop and trod heavily up the stairs to her apartment. It had started to rain, and the wind had picked up. It was a miserable day.

Running on remote, she unzipped her black, calf-high boots, kicked them into the small closet, then curled up on the couch with a blanket.

Fear clung to her, a fear that she would never find a man who could make her forget Nate McMann. The thought depressed her. And now, to find out he'd lied to her! She was furious and sad, and felt betrayed. She was so full of conflicting emotions that she could barely function.

The man had promised her the beautiful life she'd wanted, only to take all those promises away, had betrayed her far worse than she'd believed. All these years, she'd not been able to get him out of her mind, was unable to figure out what she'd done to make him not love her anymore. And all these years he'd been lying.

How could he not have told her he couldn't have children? How could he decide she didn't have the right to know something so important?

The pain he must have been in when he'd found that out. Nate loved children. He'd wanted as many children as she had. The news must have devastated him.

Still, to lie to her like that… How little he must have thought of her.

How much he must have loved you.

No! She swallowed the lump that had lodged in her throat and angrily brushed a tear off her cheek. She was not going to cry.

She wasn't. Really, she wasn't.

She had to be strong. She would move forward.

She'd gotten through this once and she'd get through it again.

Maybe knowing what she knew now would help her get past this shadow Nate had thrown across her path, blocking her from falling in love with any other man. Maybe now she could finally allow herself to have the man and family she'd always wanted.

Nate couldn't have children.

She closed her eyes. None of it made sense. What had happened? The doorbell rang, so unexpected in the silence that Bethany jumped. Not feeling like seeing anyone, she decided to ignore it.

But it came again, this time twice. And then again. And again.

Deciding she'd better see what was going on, she hurried down the stairs and opened the door.

"You have to help me," Joleen cried, bursting past her the instant the door was opened. She wore a towel wrapped around her head with a parka over that.

"What's wrong?" Bethany asked, alarmed by the anxiety on Joleen's face.

"He asked me out! Harry really asked me out! He didn't yesterday, when I thought he might, and I was feeling really horrible. I mean, he was almost there—I could tell it—but then I didn't ask him out. And when I left the store after a bunch of kids came in, I was so disappointed. And then today, when I was coming out of my boarding house, there he was, pacing back and forth with a box of chocolates. For *me!* He asked me if I wanted to go to dinner tonight."

She rambled onward, wringing her hands and pacing back and forth as she spouted off what had happened. Now she paused and looked frantic. "I'm just so nervous that I accidentally turned the shower on when I took my bath and I soaked my hair! I don't do my own hair. I have absolutely no talent in that department, and my hairdresser is out of town! Oh, Bethany, can you help me?"

Bethany's heart went out to Joleen. She was worse than a nervous teenager getting ready for her first date. "Show me what you've got under all those layers."

Looking resigned, Joleen yanked her hood off first, then the towel.

Her usually perfect blond helmet was plastered, half-dry, to her head. Bethany took one look, locked her arm in Joleen's and headed them up the stairs. "Come on, my friend, and let's get you ready for this date. I'm not the best with a blow-dryer and a curling iron, but I'm sure I can help you."

"I hope so," Joleen cried. "This is my big chance."

"Nope. It's not," Bethany said, leading her into her bathroom and pulling out the vanity stool. "This is Harry's chance. The man would be a number-one fool not to fall madly in love with you. You're a treasure." She gently pushed Joleen to sit, and met her gaze in the mirror.

Joleen stared at her reflection. "I hope Harry thinks so. I'm just so nervous I don't know if I can even talk. What if I don't talk?"

Bethany laughed and reached for her blow-dryer. "Relax, Joleen. Just be yourself and he's going to love you."

The way Bethany felt right now, if he didn't, she just might have to go over there and put a knot on his head.

Joleen's hair was very fine, and Bethany found a great respect for the hair stylist that coaxed it into a style and got it to stay. Struggling a little, Bethany curled it with the curling iron, only to have it fall limply.

"See, I can't get it to do anything," Joleen moaned, biting her lip.

Determination filled Bethany. She would put a smile on Joleen's face *and* a curl in her hair. Bethany didn't have to use a lot of hair products on her own hair, but she did have hair spray. Grabbing it, she doused Joleen's hair, then picked up the curling iron and met Joleen's gaze in the mirror.

"This will work," she assured her, and then clamped the hot iron to a swath of fine, blond hair. The hair sizzled ominously, but to Bethany's relief it didn't stick to the metal. And when she brushed the hair, it retained some curl—but…

"Oh, no," she gasped, getting a whiff of scorched hair. "Do you smell that?" It was awful! She felt awful! What had she done?

Joleen sniffed, touched a curl and to Bethany's surprise gave her a big, bright smile. "Oh, don't you mind a bit about that," she said, waving her red-tipped hand. "You got some curl in it, *girrrl,* and that is what counts. My perfume will knock that itty-bitty burnt scent right out of there."

Bethany chuckled and felt better. "See, there, that's what I'm talking about. You just go out there and be your sweet, wonderful self, and everything is going to be perfect. I just know it."

In the end, she was able to give Joleen a style similar to what she normally wore, though it wasn't exactly as stiff as usual. It was actually a softer look for her.

"I love it," Joleen said, giving her a big

hug. "You will never know how much this means to me."

When she left, it was with a calmer spirit and high *hopes*.

Bethany prayed as she watched her new friend leave. *Please, Lord, please let this be a great first date for Joleen and Harry.*

He loved her. Nate drove out of town slowly. His heart told him to turn his truck around and go back and get Bethany to see that what he'd done had been for her. Yes, he'd lied, no other word for it…it had bothered him all these years, but he'd talked himself out of feeling wrong by believing he'd done what was right for Bethany. But had he?

She should have been given the right to make up her own mind. Even if it had been rejecting him. Had that been what he was most afraid of?

The idea slammed into him. He never really addressed that point. He'd made his decision based on her giving up her dreams of success and of children, because she loved him so much. But what if she'd not chosen him? What if she'd sat back and taken in the entire picture and realized that the best thing for her to do was to make the smart decision and leave him behind? The very idea, just the thought of her rejection, knocked the wind out of him.

Had it been arrogance on his part to think that she would have taken pity on him and chosen to stay? Or that she could have loved him despite his inability to father her children.

Nate pressed the brake and pulled his truck to the side of the road. She had a point… *"If you had loved me, you would have believed enough in me to trust me to make the decision that was right for me."*

No, he'd loved her. He'd loved her with all his heart and soul—*still* loved her with every fiber of his being. There just was no way that wasn't the truth, but he should have given her the choice—trusted her to make her own decision.

Trusted her to walk away from him, if that was what her decision might have been. All these years she'd felt rejected.

Nate crossed his arms over the steering wheel and dropped his forehead to rest on them. How would he have felt if it had been he who had been rejected?

How had he missed that?

Dear Lord, I did take the easy way out.

The knowledge hurt and shamed him.

When the doorbell rang at nine-thirty, Bethany's heart kicked up. Had Nate come back?

After Joleen left, she'd been restless and confused. Had she been too hard on Nate? The look on his face when she accused him of not loving her hadn't phased her during the height of the moment. Now, given time to reflect, it was as clear as day. He'd believed he'd been doing the right thing. Did it matter, looking back now, that she thought he was wrong?

His choice hurt. It crushed her, really. But could she forgive him?

Hurrying downstairs, she pulled the door opened. Joleen stood there dabbing her teary eyes. "Oh, Bethany, it was horrible. Just horrible!"

Alarmed, Bethany took Joleen's arm and gently pulled her inside. "Come on," she said gently. "Come upstairs and let me fix you a hot cup of tea, and you tell me what was so horrible."

"Oh, Bethany, I couldn't talk. I knocked my tea over, I was so nervous. When I did talk, I was like a bumbling idiot! And he wouldn't talk. It made me terribly nervous and I rambled and rambled and rambled," she rambled.

Hugging her, Bethany led her back up the stairs. "It's going to be okay, Joleen. I know it is. You were both nervous. That's all."

"No." Joleen said, sniffling as she sank into the kitchen chair Bethany pulled out for her. "He's been hurt, betrayed by the person he loved. He just can't move forward, even after all this time." She sniffed. "I was betrayed by my husband, so I can understand his hesitancy." She sighed. It was a sigh packed full of pain and loss.

Bethany grabbed two cups and filled them with water, then stuck them in the microwave while listening intently to

Joleen. "I'm so sorry." Bethany thought of Nate and how she'd felt betrayed by him.

Joleen dried her tears. "Don't be. I'm okay, I'm stronger than I look and I'm trying to move forward. I—well—I've forgiven my ex and am trying to move on. I'm just not having much luck. I got my hopes up with Harry…I really thought coming here would be a good thing. I mean, all these fine, strong men… Honestly, that article was right on the money about them being hunks. Why, gracious me, just look at your Nate. That cowboy is so strong and handsome, and looks like he would ride in and save the day. You know what I mean—he's got the look—steadfast, *I'm your man* kind of look, and it's all directed at you, Bethany. That's something to cherish. That's something to grab hold of like it was Klondike gold, and never, never let go of—believe me, that's the treasure in life, and it isn't easily found."

Bethany wanted to deny it all, but she couldn't. Nate *did* have that look. He always had. And when he looked at her, she always—always—felt exactly the way Joleen had just described it.

But he'd betrayed her.

The microwave dinged. Lost in thought, she opened the door, pulled the cups out and dropped the teabags into the water.

He hadn't meant to betray you.

"Bethany, are you all right?"

Turning, she smiled at Joleen. "This is about you, Joleen. Are *you* all right?"

Joleen looked kindly at her with her big brown eyes. "No, honey, today you have been about the best friend I've had in a really long time. I've come here crying on your shoulder, and you've been so wonderful to me, and it has suddenly dawned on me that you look like you could use a friend. What's happened? I know I talk a lot, but believe it or not, honey, I *really* am a good listener."

Bethany didn't think she could sleep after Joleen headed back to her boarding house around the corner, but she did. She was exhausted.

Joleen *was* a great listener. Bethany told her everything, how Nate had told her he didn't love her to cover up the news that he couldn't have children, because he thought he was doing what was right by her. She told her how it hurt and how she'd struggled all these years, trying to move on, and that she hadn't been able to. She told her how Nate's larger-than-life shadow had loomed over every relationship she'd tried to have. And again, how betrayed she felt.

Joleen reminded her that he was a man— that he sounded like the kind of man who wanted to do right. Bethany agreed. That was exactly how he was. He lived by a code of honor, and she loved him for the way he was.

If she loved him for the way he was, had she put him on a pedestal? Joleen had asked her that. Did she not think that, whether she agreed or not with what he'd done, she should forgive him simply on the basis that he'd done what that code and his heart had led him to do? That, yes, in Bethany's heart, she hadn't agreed, and from Bethany's point of view, it had been the wrong way to handle it—but that was something that couldn't be changed.

Bethany had stared at Joleen and nodded. These were the facts, and nothing—no explaining, no anything—could ever change that.

Joleen had stood and given her a really hard hug, leaned back, looked into Bethany's eyes and said, "If this is the case, then nothing will ever change what happened in the past. So you, Bethany, have to decide if you are going to let that continue to hold you back. You need to decide if you still love Nate McMann. If you do—then what are you going to do about it?"

Bethany was still thinking about everything the next morning, when she left her apartment and walked downstairs to the shop. God was dealing with her in a heavy way as she moved inside and turned on the lights. What did she want?

She did love Nate. Always had.

Bethany flipped on the switch of her computer and her e-mail alert signaled that she had mail. Absently, she clicked the mouse and saw something from Shelly. It was a picture of Cody, smiling and hugging a puppy. Her heart tugged at the sight of the little boy.

The door of the shop opened and Casey Donner poked her head inside. "Hi, Bethany, I know I'm supposed to be meeting with you this morning, but I need to reschedule. All the tour guides and I have been called in for an emergency meeting right now. Penelope Lear is missing. They're about to man a search for her."

Bethany thought of the pretty woman and gasped. "How long?"

Casey looked serious "She hasn't been back to her hotel since Saturday morning."

"That was the morning I saw her buying supplies for a trip into the wilderness."

"That's what they've figured out. They think she went on a hike by herself and never returned. I have to run."

Bethany hurried to the sidewalk and watched Casey run across the street and toward the tour company. As she watched, she saw tour guides pulling into the parking lot and heading inside. This was serious. A woman like Penelope had no business out there alone. None. The danger was high this late in October, with the weather turning. She saw Nate and her heart kicked in. He hopped from the truck, his face grave. His hat low over his eyes, he flipped his coat collar up and glanced her way. Even at this distance, his blue eyes pierced her heart.

She was walking before she realized it. He didn't move, just stood by his truck and watched her. What was she doing? The question clanged in her head as she hurried across the street.

Going to get the man I love, that's what!

"Nate," she gasped, breathless from the near-freezing air burning her lungs. She didn't have on her coat, she realized, as the air cut through her sweater. She didn't care. He was going on a search-and-rescue mission. She knew he was excellent at what he did, but anytime he went into the wilderness there was danger. There was always the chance that something could happen and he might not return. She knew she had to speak to him.

She was startled when he opened his arms to her. Without hesitation she stepped into them. "I love you, Bethany. I always have and I always will. I'm so sorry. I know you can't forgive me, but I wish you could—"

"No, *I'm* sorry. I was too hard on you. There is nothing to forgive. You did what your heart told you to do. And I'm doing what mine tells me to do right now. I love you, Nate. I want you and our children. Please tell me you still want that."

He looked at her as if she'd slapped him. "I can't—"

"Yes, you can. I'm convinced that God put us on that tour with Cody to show us His plan for us. He has a child, or children, out there for us to adopt. But even if we can't, I understand that my life will never be complete without you in it. God brought me full circle, back to where you are. Back to where my heart is. Nate, I want to spend my life with you."

Joleen had told her she needed to go after what she wanted, and that was exactly what Bethany was doing. And it felt so right. So perfectly, wonderfully right, as she spoke the words. And watching Nate's eyes light up reassured her of his feelings.

"I love you, Bethany Marlow—have never stopped loving you. I have made the worst mistakes of my life, where decisions about you were concerned. But in doing that, I never once meant to hurt you. I only wanted what was best for you."

"I understand that now. I've made mistakes, too, where we're concerned, and I'm sure we will both make more. But, if we love each other and we vow to be open and honest with our communication from here on out, and work together like God wants us to, then we can overcome anything together."

Nate hugged her tight. "Are you sure?"

Bethany nodded.

"You'd better be, because this is the only

chance I'm giving you to back out of marrying me."

She laughed. "Mr. McMann, you're stuck with me for the rest of your life."

"Bethany, darlin', I love you with all my heart and soul." He dropped to his knee, right there in the parking lot.

Bethany gasped as the cold wind hit her full force, but she didn't care. Nate was looking up at her with the most gorgeous smile—one that instantly warmed her from the inside out.

"Bethany, will you marry me?"

All these years. All that time.

"Yes."

It was a simple word that held such marvelous promise...such new beginnings.

"Yes!" Nate grabbed her off the ground and spun once, then his lips found hers and he kissed her with so much heart that, as far as she was concerned, all the cold in Alaska disappeared.

"Come on, darlin'," he said too soon. "I need to get you out of this cold and go help locate this Penelope Lear."

"I'll help, too," Bethany said, as he took her hand and they started toward the building. The snow had started to fall as they kissed, and the soft flakes felt like icy feathers as they landed on her face.

Glancing at Nate, her heart was so full of love—and confidence. That *Now Woman* magazine article had been right when it called all the guides from Alaska's Treasures tours hunky—but they were so much more than that. They were experienced, capable and heroic men of the Yukon, if anyone could find the treasure to save the town, they would. But more important, this lost woman—if she really was lost—could count her blessings, because these men were the best men for the job of finding her and bringing her home safe…. Bethany said a prayer as Nate held open the door for her. She looked into his eyes, thanked God he was hers, and together, they went inside to the warmth.

The place was packed. Reed and Gage were at the back with the maps, and everyone was gathered around them. This was real.

"We still need to be on the lookout for Tucker while we're out there," Reed was saying.

Jake was standing beside Alex, looking grim. "I know time is running out," he said. "But I feel like there's still hope for Tucker. He knows this country. This woman doesn't. Time is of the essence."

"The conditions are getting worse out there," Reed said. "You'll all need to be extra careful. We don't want to lose anyone. We only want to bring Tucker and Penelope home."

"Oh, Nate, you'll be careful."

Nate turned to Bethany. "I need to tell you this before everything gets crazy. I want to adopt a houseful of children with you, if possible. You need to know that I want you to have everything you've ever dreamed of. I realize that the town might never find the treasure it's looking for, but this, right here, is the important stuff. I'm going out there, and if God's willing, we're going to find

Penelope and Tucker. But rest assured that I'm coming back to you. God has blessed me with a true treasure in your love, and nothing can stop me from coming back to marry you and starting out life together at last."

Bethany put her arms around his neck and kissed him again. "And I'll be waiting," she murmured against his lips.

Somewhere behind them, she heard Amy's smiling voice. "Well, it's about time, you two."

She was right, it was.

* * * * *

Dear Reader,

I hope you enjoyed *Yukon Cowboy*. I've never worked on a continuity before but I enjoyed working with the other authors on this project. I loved researching Alaska! What a beautiful place it is.

Bethany and Nate really had a problem. But even before Nate broke off their relationship they were headed for trouble because, though they were in love, their life goals didn't match up. I enjoyed exploring their situation and I hope you enjoyed watching them come to understand each other. I always enjoy seeing where God leads me in reconciling my characters' differences.

Now that I've finished *Yukon Cowboy* it's time for me to leave Treasure Creek and return home to my Mule Hollow series. I sure hope you'll come visit me there when *Yuletide Cowboy* hits the shelves in December 2010. Goodness, God has been good this year—it's been busy and full of ups and downs but God is always, always steadfast and sure! I pray God gives you blessings and peace in all that you do.

I love hearing from readers. Please contact me at debraclopton.com or P.O. Box 1125 Madisonville, Texas 77864.

Until next time, live, laugh and seek God with all your hearts.

Debra Clopton

QUESTIONS FOR DISCUSSION

1. As a teenager Bethany had big dreams and believed she could have it all. If Nate hadn't called off their relationship what do you think would have happened to them?

2. Given the circumstances, do you think Nate did the right thing? Or do you think he acted rashly?

3. Bethany told him, when the truth finally came out, that she didn't think he loved her at all since he didn't trust her enough to tell her the truth and let her make her own decision. What do you think?

4. Why had Bethany distanced herself from God? Have you done this?

5. What do you think about Delilah? Have you ever known anyone like her?

6. What do you think about Joleen? Have you ever known anyone like her?

7. What do you think is the difference between Delilah and Joleen?

8. Nate was raised to be a man of honor, and yet he felt like his father hadn't been totally honorable in the way he'd treated his grandfather. Being honorable in every situation is hard because people make mistakes. Do you think honor is disappearing from our society? Why or why not?

9. Jesus was the only perfect, completely honorable man who ever walked the earth. Does knowing and understanding this make forgiving others who fail you easier?

10. When Nate realized that he'd taken the easy way out by not giving Bethany a choice, he is upset. What had he been afraid of? Her rejection? Or her pity?

11. When he put the shoe on the other foot and thought about how he would have felt had she done the same thing to him, what did he feel? What would you have felt?

12. Bethany found her way back to a personal relationship with God partly through praying for Joleen. Why is that? Do you think serving others and being concerned for others helps us put things into perspective? Why or why not?

13. What about this book hit home with you the most? Discuss this with your group.

14. Have you ever been distant from God? What circumstance pushed you away from God? What pulled you back to Him?

15. Were you happy with how Nate and Bethany worked their problems out? Why or why not?

LARGER-PRINT BOOKS!

GET 2 FREE LARGER-PRINT NOVELS PLUS 2 FREE MYSTERY GIFTS

Larger-print novels are now available...